HIGH RISE

VANESSA LEE

Cover illustration Shannon Barwell
Cover layout Victoria Heath Silk
Interior design by Amie McCracken

"You are not a drop in the ocean,
you are the ocean in a drop."

Rumi
(Persian poet from the 13th Century)

PROLOGUE. GUIL

The tourists enter Bombora memorial park at the appointed time and follow the curved path south. Fields of grass and wild-flowers stretch away to the right, dipping down towards the bay, while the expanse of the Pacific Ocean shimmers to the left. A cluster of ink green pine trees creates a pool of shade in front of them, their spicy smell intoxicating in the heat. It is silent except for the tourists' feet grinding into the fine pebbles of the path and the thrum of cicadas.

A large blue and white pontoon bobs under a rock shelf in the distance. The silhouette of a tall, shirtless man waits with his arms crossed and feet planted wide. He waves a welcome, his long and toned arm stencilled black against the porcelain blue sky.

On approach, they are surprised to see the man is much older than he had appeared from a distance. His heavily tanned skin drapes his bones like fine crepe, a multitude of tiny dark freckles covering his limbs. His thick curls, caked with salt, glint in the sun like silver coins stashed behind his ears. As he extends a hand to help each passenger down onto the gently bobbing pontoon, the ropey muscles of his shoulders twitch. He has a strong and steady grip, impressive for a man his age.

"I'm Guil. Welcome to Bombora."

Guil's snorkelling tour has taken on the macabre allure previously seen at sites such as Chernobyl and is always fully booked with a waiting list of at least eight weeks. Three tours of fifteen people are easily filled every Saturday. He holds a monopoly, being the sole holder of a permit to conduct business in what is now a memorial park, having solid connections to the previous local council of Bombora.

He provides masks and snorkels, short sleeved wetsuits (for buoyancy only, the water is always comfortably warm) and underwater cameras. Posing underwater on the submerged park benches is one of the main attractions. Even better are the photos you can take seated at one of the tables in the drowned restaurant, Vaga, although only the more dextrous snorkellers can manage to "sit" in one of the seats that has been bolted to a concrete slab.

In good weather and calm water, the submerged Vaga shimmers with its original tiles in colours reminiscent of coral. The bar that has once held a curvy La Marzocco coffee machine is still there, having been constructed in cement. That is also a popular shot with the punters; leaning on the still-tiled bar, pretending to hold a delicate espresso cup, little finger held high, laughing behind the snorkel and sending coils of tiny white bubbles streaming to the surface.

After they have suited up and entered the water, Guil allows his customers ten minutes or so to explore the cavern of the restaurant and take their photos, then indicates they should follow him a little north along the curve of the old beach promenade. There, they hover over two curved, aluminium benches sitting together in silent and eerie companionship. These benches, which once provided generations of bottoms a resting place and the perfect vantage point from which to eat hot chips and watch the waves, now provide — at best — visibility of one metre into the plankton-filled, effervescent waters of the Pacific Ocean.

They kick languidly in the water to follow him until they are hovering above a crumbling three-sided stone wall. An old chain is draped in long curves atop each side — two short, one long — which glint dully through the soft green algae that grows between the links. The rock pool. The three flat stone steps that had led down from the Esplanade to the pool are still evident, even though many years of incoming and outgoing tides have deposited enough sand over them to blunt their edges.

After allowing the snorkellers time to drift above all three sides of the rock pool on a vigilant lookout for the infamous blue ringed octopus, Gull indicates that they should head back towards the pontoon. They kick back, again tracing the curve of the beach promenade. Some of the more observant snorkellers spot a rusty row of bike racks which are almost obscured by clumps of swaying seaweed.

Clambering up into the pontoon is often emotional if there are tourists who had lived in Bombora or who have relatives who did. Masks are pulled off faces and the exclamations begin.

"I have a photo of my grandmother holding me as a baby in front of that rock pool!"

"My earliest memory is of sitting on that beach wall and dropping my ice cream into the sand."

"My hen's night was at Vaga. I got so drunk on tequila I have never touched a drop since."

Guil does not join in and share his stories. He does, however, have a small folder of laminated photos that he hands around at the end of his tour. He silently sips from a thermos of coffee while his customers leaf through the folder, grinning or sighing in turns at the images of families spread out on towels on the sand, or queuing for hot chips at the kiosk. There is an extraordinary image of a man hauling a half-metre long baby Port Jackson shark from the rock pool and throwing it over the edge back into the ocean.

"I wasn't there, but I know the man in that photo," Guil answers when asked. "His name was Mick."

There is another photo that always prompts curious questions. It is the last photo in the folder, blown up to a larger size than the rest. A young, lean surfer stands with his wetsuit pulled down around his narrow hips and grasps a surfboard with his left arm. His other arm is around an older woman who shares his tanned skin and thick wavy hair. She wears a yellow sundress with thin straps and a long skirt that billows around her ankles and she balances an oversized wicker beach basket on her shoulder. Anyone can recognise that she looks at the young man with motherly pride. Behind them, the blue block letters spelling out "Vaga" on the wall of the restaurant behind them are clearly visible.

All Guil says when asked is, "Yes, that was my mother. Renata."

Then he points at the box to indicate where everyone should throw their masks and snorkels, and he turns his back and busies himself with the preparations for the next tour.

CHAPTER 1. BOMBORA

Mick kicked off his thongs and walked barefoot over the pine needle-strewn path down to the beach. There was an incoming tide and the salt haze shimmered in the air; the figures of lean, after-school surfers swooped in the marble-coloured foam. Small children in their school uniforms hopped up and down the broad concrete steps separating the promenade from the sand, balancing dripping ice blocks and trying to keep the neon drips from their pale blue collared shirts. Mothers admonished from a distance, huddled together in a group in front of the surf lifesaving club, sipping on their lattes and green goddess juices and organising the next day's driving rosters to netball games and rugby training.

"Hey Mick! Looking spiffy!" One mother, who had removed her t-shirt and was reclining on her elbows on the yellow stairs of the club, pushing her sunburned and freckled chest to the sky, smiled at Mick as he passed. Her white, fringed bikini top barely covered her breasts, and her tanned legs stretched out under the denim cut-offs she wore. The other women pivoted to see who she was calling out to.

"Mick!"

"G'day, Mick!" went up the cries, and he nodded shyly and waggled a hand limply, still swinging his shoes in the other hand.

He could not have correctly identified any of these women, not only because their faces were obscured by oversized sunglasses, or because they all looked completely interchangeable — the same bleached hair, the same cut-offs, the same belly button piercings sparkling in the mild afternoon sun — he genuinely did not know who they were. If Sam, his wife, were with him she would at least be able to greet a couple by name. These women were a good few years older than their own grown children, so it was fair to say they were not part of that tight group of kids, dear to his heart, who had spent hours in his home overlooking Patriot Bay, taking the stand-up paddle boards and Jet Skis out onto the sparkling waters after school and on weekends. He was sure he did not know these women, and yet at the same time was unsettled that maybe he did know at least some of them but just could not place them. This helpless feeling of not being able to recall details at will had been troubling him more and more lately.

It was feasible that Mick had either employed one of their husbands or boyfriends, or had rented an apartment to them at one point, or they may have been at one of the numerous fundraising events that he and Sam had held over the years at the yacht club. As he got older, though, the over-familiarity of such people was getting on his nerves, the constant pressure to hold the entire interconnected community of Bombora straight in his head. The strain of staying on top of who was married to whom, whose sister had cancer, whose children had moved overseas, who had defaulted on a loan, who had slipped a disc, who had moved to Bega, who had won thousands on the greyhounds, who was renovating their back deck, whose child had just been signed up to the Bombora Eagles junior rugby team. So despite the faces of these young mothers still swivelled towards him, waiting for a reply or an explanation of where he was going freshly shaved and in a neatly ironed shirt — "Got a hot date, Mick?" — he lowered his chin and hurried the last few metres to Vaga.

Vaga. Not the fanciest of Bombora's seafood restaurants, but undoubtedly perched on the best real estate. Right next door to the art deco-inspired concrete swimming Complex which housed an indoor pool and was home to a successful swim squad (both of Mick's children had been competitive swimmers), Vaga occupied a bright, airy space — just an open box, really — covered in bright tiles of tangerine and jade and with doors that completely receded and gave the impression that you were eating right on the sand. In fact, the floor was constantly strewn with sand and it was not unheard of to wander in barefoot and order your swordfish carpaccio and a crisp glass of pinot gris without being asked to put your shoes back on. Mick, however, preferred to slip his thongs on before ducking into the cool interior. Sam would not approve of him shuffling to her table shoeless. He could hear her now; "Look at you, like a hobo with your hairy Hobbit feet!"

"Micky boy! Mate!"

Lou, the broad-chested owner of Vaga, swooped on Mick and pulled his head towards his chest with enthusiasm. Mick was overcome with the smell of his armpits (hints of musky talc) mixing with fried calamari before he managed to pull free and escape the pounding back slap he was simultaneously being subjected to. Mick had helped broker the rental deal between the real estate developer and Lou, granting him an unusually long lease for the site of Vaga, and so these exuberant, almost aggressive hugs were likely to continue for eternity. Sam got the sweeter end of the deal, with glass after glass of free wine bestowed on her and her friends during their regular afternoon visits.

"The missus is over there, mate. Be with you in a sec."

Sam sat alone at a table for six, the other places strewn with napkins, grissini crumbs and empty wine glasses bearing bright lipstick smudges in shades from coral to burgundy. One small plate bore the dried remnants of tiramisu with a sad, nibbled strawberry drowning forlornly in a puddle of cream. Sam's wine glass had been freshly topped up, and her slightly bleary eyes immediately swept down to Mick's exposed feet.

Fuck, he thought, *here we go.*

But it seemed Sam was otherwise preoccupied. She let her eyes return to Mick's while he dropped into his seat.

"Nice long lunch? Where are the other girls, already gone?"

Sam had called him over an hour ago, insisting that he swing by and join them for a drink. She had sounded tense and irritated and he nervously cast his mind back over the last couple of days. Had he forgotten something important, left some domestic task undone, or inadvertently embarrassed his wife? Or was he being summoned to yet again bestow some sort of favour on one of her friends; an apprenticeship for a nephew, a loan of a boat, "mate's rates" for an event at the yacht club?

Mick was under the impression some of the other husbands had been roped in as well, and so was a little surprised to find his wife presiding over an empty table. She wet her lips in preparation to speak, but fell back into her chair as Lou descended on the table and set a tall glass of beer in front of Mick.

"Thanks, mate, thanks. Place looks great, you've cleaned up well."

"Yeah, that was a biggie, that last one."

A few weeks ago, the night of the last full moon, a king tide had swept up over the concrete steps in front of Vaga and surged up to the glass doors, one of which had cracked under the pressure and given way to the dark, salty water. This was not the first time a king tide had come up that far. In fact, it was by design that Vaga was completely and very prettily tiled — floor, walls, bar — in intricate tiles in colours reminiscent of cocktails, parrots and sunsets. It was like a massive, extravagant, Mediterranean shower cubicle filled with simple, rust proof chairs and tables that could be stacked and secured against a wall, which happened more and more often these days. Lou had trained his staff never to leave stock or equipment on the floor and had, at significant expense, invested in large, waist-height lockers for storage of everything from liquor to toilet paper.

After this most recent king tide, the glass had simply needed to be replaced, a long hose was run in from the Complex next door, and the whole cavity was rinsed out under pressure, wiped down, the chairs and tables repositioned. Business actually surged after such an event, the community rallying around their miraculous surviving restaurant, rising proverbially like a salty phoenix again and again, an element of thrilling danger around every booking made during a full moon or in the days following heavy rains up north. Other towns in Australia measured rising water levels with sticks in the main street or a sports oval; Bombora measured the effects of climate change by the extent of downtime Vaga needed after a king tide. Until now, that had been only one or two days, with the community cheerfully pitching in and helping Lou each time. The after-parties Lou threw to reopen usually earned him as much back as he would have lost in takings for a few days, especially when he cheekily added kingfish to the menu and charged double for it, renaming it King Tide Cocktail and serving it as ceviche in pretty cocktail glasses.

Lou wandered off, and Sam prepared to speak, licking her dry lips with aggressive stabs of her tongue. Her lipliner was two shades too dark but had persevered throughout the afternoon, whereas her lipstick had long since disappeared. She paused for effect and announced, "The Richards are leaving." She clicked her salmon-coloured acrylic nails on the table for emphasis. "Natalie told us today."

"Leaving …?"

"Leaving the peninsula! Selling up! They're only a few houses along from the house whose deck fell down in the last swell. They'll take any price, Nat says, they have more or less written off getting any kind of gain or even breaking even!" Sam threw her narrow frame back into the chair, the horror of her announcement, the time she had sat there holding it in waiting for Mick to arrive, now seemingly exhausting her. She squeezed her eyes together, and Mick saw a clump of dehydrated, azure mascara break free and land on the high point of her cheekbone.

"They're going? John hasn't said a word to me. I only just ran into him outside the butcher."

"Well, he wouldn't dare tell you, would he?"

"What does that mean?"

"He's scared to tell you! Everyone knows where you stand! That we all need to stay, lobby harder for … I don't know what, what are you lobbying for? For the council to sandbag the whole peninsula? I have lost track of what it is you think is going to happen. But nothing *is* going to happen!" Sam was leaning forward again, her chest dropping low and hovering over the rim of the table. One strap of her dress had slipped off her shoulder, and Mick's eyes reflexively darted to the pale moon of breast above her bra line.

"Sam, please ... Can you ...?" Mick glanced around the room and used his hand to indicate dropping the volume, although aside from Lou, who was preoccupied over by the till, they were alone.

"One by one, all my friends are leaving, Mick. At least — the ones who can *afford* to leave. Soon, all that will be left here," Sam waved a hand to indicate the empty room, still full of the debris of a long lunch trade, "will just be people with no other choice. People who can't just walk away from their mortgages, or all those *renters* in your buildings, hanging on till the bitter end because they have nothing to lose."

At the mention of "his renters", Mick stiffened. The way she hissed the word and pursed her lips, as if sucking on the rim of a salted margarita glass. As if those renters had not afforded them the lifestyle they enjoyed, including the fact that she could spend practically every afternoon in this very restaurant with her friends wearing a different imported-from-Bali dress each time.

"Nothing is going to happen to those buildings. Everyone will be safe and *they* know that. Those buildings are nowhere near where Nat and John live. Even *I* could have told them years ago that buying there was a mistake."

That was a white lie. The decades-long friendship between the two couples — Mick, Sam, John, and Nat — had rarely been marred by jealousies, but Mick had always envied the Richards's glorious position on the northern end of the long chain of Bombora beaches. Their home was set at an angle so that from their huge deck you could watch the sun sink behind the high-rises of South Bombora, the ones that housed the very "renters" that Sam now seemed to find so distasteful. When the plot of land had been announced for development more than fifteen years ago, Mick had briefly toyed with the idea of purchasing it and developing townhouses, but the council only wanted to approve single family dwellings at that exclusive end of the beach. Nat and John, with their slightly obnoxious southern Italian tastes, came to the party with plans for a flashy three-story home which the council hoped would attract similar vendors and transform that end of the beach from the old, grey sand dunes and informal rubbish tip to a new high-end enclave of cul-de-sacs, high white walls, transplanted palms, and sparkling swimming pools. No land needed to be wasted on communal spaces such as parks or playgrounds; each home would have their own pool and whirlpool, custom designed tree house or cabana, and outdoor lounge sets large enough to seat at least sixteen. The only communal property was a small car park on the northernmost tip with a white path that curved gently to the sand, and a bin to collect the steaming plastic bags of dog shit from early morning canine "walkies". The beach was not private, but so few people bothered to hike that far from South Bombora over the hot sand that it may as well have been. The very site of the sand dunes that Mick used to enjoy as a bare-foot child, when he would slide down them inside empty boxes salvaged from outside the supermarket, was resurrected as the Cove and became the closest thing to a gated community that had ever existed on the peninsula.

It had been good while it lasted.

. . . .

Sunday afternoons in the Cove. While the trains delivered fresh visitors in droves to the more southern beaches, the Cove — best accessible by car — was an outpost of terracotta and tinted glass. The oversized houses sat politely far enough back from each other, cleverly pointing in different directions, so that from the outdoor barbeque area each family could entertain and feel like they were alone with the circling seagulls, drifting white clouds in a baby blue sky, and their guests. The wind, which whipped a little more energetically up at the point, allowed each home to blast their own playlist and gossip outrageously but barely be heard by their neighbours. While the beachgoers a little down south, slick with sunscreen, queued at the kiosks for wraps, smoothies and hot chips, the fare in the Cove was decidedly more gourmet, sometimes catered, but mostly prepared by the proud couples who loved to demonstrate their mastery of colourful Mediterranean salads, heaped with pistachios and herbs, and an assortment of fresher-than-fresh shellfish and premium marinated meats. Even Vaga could not compete with the excesses that hit the tables at the Cove on a Sunday. For a brief period over at Nat's, elegant mounds of cocaine would be left inside — away from the wind — for a late afternoon pick-me-up to ease the transition from lunch to dinner and help make sure that all that expensive food was consumed, but Nat did away with that custom after it became apparent that under those conditions, her guests would never leave.

Mick and Sam were routinely invited to several of the Cove homes, but were most often to be found lounging on the crisp white outdoor settee on Nat and John's wide deck. Sam and Nat had met as young mothers, and had also once reclined on the steps of the Complex and watched their toddlers playing in the sand. Then, of course, there were no cool cafes from which to grab wheatgrass shots or acai yoghurt cups — and definitely no Vaga at which to sip a stealthy post-school wine on a Friday — they had simply packed sandwiches, cheese sticks and water bottles for their children. The young women would let the kids tire themselves on the sand and at the water's edge, hoping this would ensure a flawless bedtime routine later, and would prolong the moment before the water bottles and buckets needed to be collected and thrown into hessian bags permanently filled with sand and tiny fragments of shell. They would grab the toddlers' sticky hands, swat sand out of the creases of their clothes, and lug everything home to start on simple evening meals of grilled lamb chops and minted peas.

They had lived in modest brick bungalows (albeit on massive blocks of land) and enjoyed what they felt were normal, suburban lives. It would not be until the nineties when property prices started escalating wildly that they found themselves launched into the enviable cohort of coastal property owners who could leverage their equity for more and more bank loans, snapping up larger chunks of the peninsula as it evolved from sleepy beachside suburb to a more exclusive, self-conscious version of itself.

Mick and John had been bullish, running in the same circle of bankers, council members, and property developers who seized on the market sentiment and constantly hatched new plans to develop more and more of the dunes, marsh and parkland into new housing. When they ran out of ground space, the race was on to build and invest in the high-rises that sprung up around the main shopping street and train station. Sam would often tease Mick that he would exhume the Heights Cemetery and personally carry the bones away if it meant access to another huge development site, and this stung because he probably would have. As they started to have more disposable cash, holidays became more far flung than the usual caravan parks at Jervis Bay or South West Rocks; now, Noosa, Hamilton Island, and Bali were achievable — sometimes even Italy or Croatia. These new destinations became inspiration for the plans and palettes of townhouses which started to appear in Bombora with the caramel and peach tones of the Mediterranean, replacing the simple red brick of the past.

During the same period, the cafes and restaurants were also transformed. Takeaway shops with rows of deep fryers pumping out hot chips, Chiko rolls and potato scallops disappeared one by one to be replaced with cafes hosting Italian espresso machines and Vitamix blenders for the array of protein-powder enriched smoothies in demand. There was no need to offer indoor seating; the temperate weather and relaxed, beach lifestyle made it completely acceptable and preferable to drink your coffee while perched on an upturned milk crate on the street. Pilates studios sprung up, and personal training clubs were launched in every park and on the sand. The Esplanade was resurfaced to allow for easier jogging while pushing a Scandinavian, thousand-dollar pram. Even the old lawn bowling club was revamped and began to serve mezze plates under a roof completely covered with ferns and hanging plants in retro macrame hangers. Gone were the days you simply bought schooners of beer and packets of chips dumped in metal bowls and sat at wobbly, sticky plastic Formica tables. The only part of Bombora that remained frozen in time were the many sleepy inlets that branched off like the bronchi of a lung from Patriot Bay until they terminated in isolated, rocky beaches deep in the national park, populated with an uncertain number of reclusive families who prided themselves on their self-sufficiency rather than conspicuous consumption.

The Bombora lifestyle became aspirational and the numbers of people wanting to move there exploded, as did Mick and John's property portfolios. The apartments were especially in high demand by the ever-growing influx of people seeking work and a safe, picturesque place to raise their families. Jobs were plentiful in all manner of professions from wait staff and personal trainers to fashion designers, boat builders, surfboard shapers, architects, psychologists, tarot card readers, landscape gardeners, and sous chefs. Although some locals resented Bombora's upgrade, more than happy with the one bakery and pie shop they had been going to for years for sticky finger buns and lamingtons, Bombora seemed to be able to effortlessly expand and absorb the tide of new ideas, dreams and destinies. With so much open space offered up by the beaches, bays, and national parks, and school playgrounds that were large enough to house clusters of Moreton Bay fig trees under which the students could hide from the bright midday sun, the newcomers were absorbed seamlessly.

Mick and John's fortunes had boomed with Bombora's and were completely intertwined. So when Sam announced that Nat and John had decided to leave, there was much more than sentimentality in the sudden squeezing sensation in Mick's guts. There was fear, and a very uncharacteristic stab of betrayal.

CHAPTER 2. TIDE TURNS

Sam stood at her kitchen island considering her dinner options, her stomach feeling acidic and uncomfortable after the long lunch. She had changed from her floral dress into her usual yoga ensemble which she rarely did yoga in. A slight throb behind her eyes kicked in and she wondered if a small, cold glass of sauvignon blanc would fix that. She swung open the heavy fridge door and surveyed its contents. Both her children would be staying for dinner, and she had two omnivores, one pescetarian, and one vegan to deal with. On a normal night this would be a challenge, and she had risen to that challenge many times. However, on an evening such as this, with an afternoon of drinking behind her, together with the shock of Nat's news, this seemed like an insurmountable hurdle.

She had seen the shoes of both children in the entrance hall so she knew they were around somewhere. Perhaps they had jumped on their stand-up paddle boards and were enjoying a sunset tour up to the mouth of the bay and back. The tide was coming in, meaning they would have struggled on the way out, but they would surely be enjoying the sensation of being pushed gently back in towards their jetty while the sun mercifully dipped behind the horizon after what had been a scorching day. Having become much better friends as adults than they had been as teenagers, they might even both be sitting astride their boards and using the now-rare opportunity to compare notes on life; Adele was studying medicine at Sydney University, living in a Newtown terrace with an old school friend, and Ethan was finishing a gap year after which he planned to move to London and study architecture. Adele and Ethan both had boyfriends and this gave them an incredibly useful topic to bond over; depending on the day they might be found cackling over gross "boy habits" they could not contend with, or genuinely commiserating after what they had experienced as gaslighting or cold behaviour. Thankfully her children had left their partners at home; neither Sam's fridge contents nor her patience were large enough for them tonight.

Mick came in smelling of his tea tree shower gel, cheeks ruddy from steam.

"What's the plan for dinner?"

"The plan is, my dear, we ask the kids which takeaway they would like when they get back from wherever they are, and you go grab it."

Mick watched Sam knead her fingertips between her brows. He reached above his head and extracted a wine glass from an overhead cabinet.

"Sauv blanc or pinot gris?"

From outside they heard their kids laughing while they mounted the jetty from their boards. Mick wandered barefoot to their back deck and took in the sight of them. Adele, lean and tanned, wore a sleek black long-sleeved rash shirt, her thick wavy hair piled high on top of her head. She had already climbed up onto the jetty, holding her board in place with her oar, while ripping off the Velcro strap from around her ankle with a loud, wet sound that carried up to Mick on the deck.

Ethan bobbed on his board slightly off the jetty, cross-legged like a meditating monk in an oversized hoodie. The kids were so confident in their boarding skills that they often went in normal street clothes, or pyjamas. Ethan hung back calmly, waiting for his sister to haul up her board and drag it towards the little white boat shed. Mick could not help watching Ethan with concern, trying to discern if he was moving in the slow, stoned way of his youth. To his knowledge, Ethan did not smoke anymore and had cut back his drinking too, but Mick knew from experience how easy it was to cover up bad habits when needed.

"Come up kids, we're ordering in! And make sure you shut the boat shed door properly. The Kennedy's cat got stuck in there last week for three days."

When everyone had congregated around the kitchen island, Sam grabbed a handful of takeaway menus from a drawer and dumped them onto the marble slab of the island.

"Knock yourselves out. We can even get it all delivered with Uber. I am knackered."

"Honestly I would be happy with some crackers and cheese. And some of that wine." Ethan grabbed himself a glass and perched on a bar stool. Mick slid the open bottle over to him. His son was looking a little chunky, he thought, although under that huge hoodie it was impossible to tell. His face did look bloated, especially compared to Adele whose complexion was glowing and taut.

"I need to eat. I skipped lunch today." Adele scanned a Thai menu and went straight to the vegetarian section.

"Ummmm … tofu Pad Thai would be great. No egg."

Ethan scoffed. "That's hardly a Pad Thai then, is it?"

Adele pointedly ignored her brother. "Dad? You eating?"

"Order a Pad Thai with prawn for me. I'll pop out and get it." Mick wandered off and found his shoes under a chair in the living room.

"I think I will skip tonight as well," sighed Sam. "I had a pretty big lunch. But, honey, just check we have enough wine."

Jesus, thought Mick, *when have we ever not had enough wine?* With the double-doored fridge in the kitchen, plus a spare fridge downstairs next to the laundry, *and* the small bar fridge in the outdoor undercover barbeque area — all stocked with Sam's favourites from the Adelaide Hills and Barossa Valley — there was enough wine to see them through to Christmas. Next Christmas.

Adele dialled in their order, adding some spring rolls, as she knew her brother would have the munchies later and would be on the hunt for any fried food available. From outside, the mechanical whir of the garage door opening could be heard, followed by the purr of Mick's car reversing up the steep driveway.

"So, Mum, why so tired?" Adele reached for a wine glass, but only poured herself a small amount of sauvignon and topped up her glass with sparkling water.

"Oh, you know, lunch at Vaga. Like every Friday." Sam grabbed a box of crackers from the walk-in pantry and extracted a block of cheese from the fridge, placing it all in front of Ethan with a small, sharp knife and a cutting board. This was surprisingly relaxed for Sam, who typically had three different kinds of homemade dip, olives, and charcuterie ready in the fridge for any company, family or otherwise. Entertaining was her job, and she usually did it with full-blown commitment.

"Like every day, you mean," teased Adele. "Who did you go with? Jenny, Rachel? Nat?"

"Yes, all of them were there, and some other ladies you don't know. Actually, I am still a bit in shock. Nat told me they are moving." Sam's voice caught with a sharp intake of breath, as if she had swallowed a shard of glass.

"What? That's huge. They are, like, Bombora *royalty*. Where are they going?"

"I don't think they even know yet, and they may be planning to travel for a while before they choose a place to settle. But she just wanted to tell us herself. There have been a lot of rumours about the homes up there."

"So they are going to sell their McMansion up in the Cove?" Ethan had crumbs stretching from his three-day old stubble down to the logo on his hoodie. "Jesus, would anyone even want something so tacky? It's so 1990s."

"Well that's the thing. You know the last king tide we had? Their neighbours — the Henley's — lost their back deck. The whole ground under their pool also shifted and they will probably have to rip that out too, and either stabilise it all or just not bother. It's really rattled them, and they apparently just want to cut their losses and get out."

"Doesn't John have a lot of investments with Dad? What does that mean for him?"

"No idea. Your father and John have not spoken. I was the one who told Dad this afternoon."

"Well they did build a house on a sand dune!" declared Ethan, shaking more crackers out the box. "Wasn't there a warning about that in the Bible, about building a house on shifting sand …"

All three giggled at the ludicrousness of Ethan quoting the Bible to anyone.

Sam bit down gently on a cracker. "Last time I was up there, maybe a few weeks ago for book club, I was spooked by how empty it was. I couldn't see the lights on at many places at all. When I think back on how lively it used to be. Day parties, night parties, weekend-long parties. You could barely find a spot in the little visitor's car park."

Adele frowned. "You mean you think people have already started selling up? Surely you would see signs? Or you would hear through the community that a property has been listed? I mean, this is still a super competitive property market."

"My guess is that the people selling either want to keep it quiet, or have been asked to keep it quiet. Or they realise that they won't get a great price and are thinking about options."

"Options such as …?"

"Maybe it makes more sense to rent them out, or list them on those exclusive holiday rental sites. But selling under these conditions is not ideal."

Ethan grabbed another cube of cheese. "These conditions?"

Adele sighed with exasperation. "Bro, haven't you been listening? The Cove is sitting on the most vulnerable part of the shoreline around here. I have been waiting for the whole thing to fall into the sea. Every time it rains hard, I think about it. I had actually been meaning to call you after the last king tide, Mum, and ask about Nat, but I got distracted."

"You think John will just walk away? Can they afford to do that?" Ethan, a designer through and through, had by now cut an entire block of cheddar into precise cubes and arranged them into an impressively stable pyramid directly atop the pale marble island. "If I only had some carrot sticks …" he muttered to himself.

"As you said, he has a lot of other investments with Dad, mostly down around the train station and some commercial property at Devlin Point. So yes, they can afford it, although it must sting. If it wasn't for the coastline and these weather events their house would go for *millions* right now. And Nat *loves* that house. She would only ever sell it very reluctantly. I know her taste is a bit special and definitely not for everyone, but it is stunning, and my God — the view!"

"I heard she threw some nice parties back in the day. Shame kids were never invited." Sam caught Adele and Ethan exchanging a look. Ethan snickered from behind his cheese construction, and Adele lifted one eyebrow slightly and glanced sideways at her mother.

Sam shifted on her feet. Her children must have seen herself and Mick come home looking a little worse for wear over the years. Back then it was easy to justify — all her friends were doing it. Now she felt a flutter of embarrassment in her belly, especially given the issues that Ethan would go on to have with dope and god knows what else in his last years of school.

"You were already old enough to entertain yourselves on the weekend. Besides, you *hated* coming places with me and Dad back then. We would leave you here with plenty of food and you were happy as Larry. In fact, a birdie told me *you* used to have some pretty crazy parties here as well." She looked pointedly at Ethan, who was taking another slug of cold wine.

She remembered when Mick had shown her the architectural plans for their last renovation, specifically pointing out the separate entrances. "And this, clearly, is the main entertaining area, but up here ..." he tapped his finger on the large, unfurled plan, "... the kids can hang out here with their friends. And look! This door here goes down into the garage. *Their* friends can come and go without disturbing us."

It had seemed such a luxury, all that space, so much privacy for everyone. How could they have predicted that there would come a time when they kept the garage door permanently locked and the keys stashed in their bedroom safe so that they would have a better oversight of when Ethan was coming and going and with whom he was associating? There would be long nights where Sam would lie in bed, praying to hear the sounds of her son returning home safely through the front door, longing to hear him in the kitchen loudly making himself a snack and trampling through the elegant living room. There were many weekends when they would forgo entertaining and enjoying their private "adult space", so extravagantly designed and furnished, because they never knew when Ethan might come home and cause a scene, or a phone call would come that he needed to be urgently picked up from a random location which might be a private home, a dark playground, the loading zone behind Woolworths supermarket, a gutter.

"So what do you think Dad's going to do? If John is out, what does that exactly mean?" asked Ethan, lazily poking at one of the cubes of cheese in the bottom row of his pyramid. He was playing dairy Jenga.

Sam sighed and took another sip of her wine. Her mind flashed back to the last time Mick felt someone had crossed him in a business deal. He had kept a fresh roll of dollar coins, direct from the bank, in the glove box of his car at all times. When Sam had asked why, he had shown her how smoothly he could grip and conceal that roll in his fist. "One day, I'm going to see him walking along the street. He can't hide from me forever. I am going to make that punch count."

Ethan suddenly poked hard against his cube of cheese, and the whole construction collapsed, perfect square chunks tumbling across the marble.

. . . .

At the same time Mick was picking up two steaming plastic containers of Pad Thai — one with tofu but no egg, the other with garlic prawns — Lou sat alone in Vaga. The dinner crowd had come and gone early, the wind having picked up, salt spray suspended in the darkening sky, the lights on the promenade glowing like the orbs in a Van Gogh painting. His staff had heaped leftover risotto and pasta into takeaway containers and hurried home, the smell of a storm in the air. Everything was orderly and scrubbed clean and nothing was left on the floor, just as instructed.

Lou poured himself a nip of whiskey over ice and threw the golden liquid back. Spread out in front of him on the table — the last one that had not been folded and stacked against the back wall — was a letter from his insurance company with this year's renewed premium. He had heard stories from up and down the coast of cafes and restaurants being denied insurance at all, so when the envelope had arrived with the sensible blue logo on the envelope he had signed with relief. "They're insuring me, thank Christ," he had thought.

And then he saw the premium.

"Are they taking the fucking piss?" he snarled into his tumbler.

When the ice of his drink had finally melted, there was one more centimetre of diluted whiskey to throw back, which he did. He hauled his considerable mass to his feet, collapsed the table, and carried it over to the neat stack his staff had prepared against the back wall. He ran a thick chain around the legs of the tables and chairs, and secured it to a hook that had been drilled deep into the concrete.

CHAPTER 3. RENATA

Guil woke to the smell of toast and his mother singing. He heard the balcony door being unlatched and slid open, releasing the sound of pounding surf into the small living room. He did not need to hear the incoming waves to know it was a gorgeous swell; he had checked the surf conditions report last night before sleeping. He needed to get out there.

Renata was struggling to unscrew the Moka pot to make coffee as her son came padding into the kitchen.

"Oh good, you can do this," she smiled and thrust it into his arms. "Damn thing is getting so old, but it makes the best coffee. You have time for one before your surf?"

"Ah, nah, actually I was going to just eat and run." He snatched a piece of buttered toast from a pile his mother had assembled on the cutting board. A small pan was simmering, waiting for eggs to be lowered in carefully. "Everyone's out there already. The waves will be too full."

Everyone. His mother pondered the word while she chewed a square of toast. Guil used to surf alone, or with one or two friends. Now he was referencing this "everyone" more and more. It seemed to her that wherever he went these days, whether surfing or out in the evening, his group was expanding. More and more names were mentioned in passing, more than Renata could possibly keep up with. Guil had never been a misfit, but he had never been an extrovert either. He had kept the same handful of friends since school, even though they both had moved away for almost four years and only recently come back to Bombora. He had slotted right back in like he had never left, but both mother and son had noticed immediately once they were back — something had shifted in Bombora.

Renata also saw it when she was out and about. There were noticeably more young people than she had ever remembered, lounging in large groups under the pine trees of Collins Park or sprawled in the sun in the main street with their wireless speakers and skateboards. Actually, she liked it; she had always felt Bombora was too much of a boomer town, with elegant couples in resort wear filling the cafes and restaurants, seemingly with no pressure to fill their days with work or chores. Those people were still around and giving the groups of kids a wide berth, setting their mouths into thin lines and pointedly avoiding eye contact when their paths crossed, as they invariably did.

Renata, on the other hand, enjoyed the spontaneous music and clamour that filled the public spaces. It reminded her of life in Portugal in a small village just north of Lisbon. Even though she had left as a young girl, she remembered how whole families had gathered at sunset outside the church; children ran barefoot, adults gossiped. No one locked themselves inside to watch television when you could be lounging on a wooden bench catching up on the day's news, the stones of the piazza glowing rose and releasing the day's heat gently back into the approaching night.

She had never been able to find that feeling of connection and community in Australia. As a consequence, evenings here had only brought melancholy, which was only easing now that she was back in Bombora, in this tiny but sun-filled apartment with views to the sea, alone with Guil — her tanned and gentle boy. High up above the Esplanade, she felt safe as Rapunzel in her tower. No one could drop by without first buzzing from downstairs, twelve floors below, and announcing themselves. The chain in the front door could be held in place until she could see exactly who was coming down the passage from the elevator to her door. For the first time in years she felt herself starting to relax, if only for small pockets of time. She would catch herself during the day doing the most banal things — wiping a counter, folding laundry — and realise her jaw was clenched, her buttocks hard as a rock. She would will herself to let go — "It's over," she would tell herself — but she remained in a near constant state of hyper alertness.

Standing in her living room, the floorboards were warm as crumpets under her feet, the sun having been streaming in since five in the morning. She had never imagined she could afford to rent an apartment in one of these high-rises facing eastwards into the horizon. Yes, it was tiny. So tiny, in fact, she could vacuum the whole apartment without unplugging the vacuum cleaner and changing to another socket. There was so little storage space, the same narrow cupboard in the hall held drinking glasses, salad bowls, Tupperware, beach towels, a wicker picnic basket, and her first aid supplies. She and Guil shared one built-in wardrobe in Guil's bedroom (the larger one), and she slept on a sofa bed in the other half-sized bedroom. They ate their meals while perched on bar stools at the kitchen counter, rather than squeeze a dining table into the living room. After all that she and Guil had been through, this felt like a luxury, and the smallness and snugness of everything was a constant reminder that she was living alone with Guil. No one else would fit. And that's exactly what she wanted.

. . . .

Guil had been gone for a few hours and the apartment was gleaming after an energetic Saturday morning clean. Renata decided to try to find her son down by the rocks where she suspected he might be lounging after his surf. She knew she would be able to lure him away for a generous brunch. Lean and athletic, food was his constant preoccupation.

The Esplanade — usually full of joggers, dog walkers and toddlers that made it impossible to walk in a straight line — was thinning out. The sun was now approaching its highest point and it beat down onto the cement beneath Renata's feet. She could feel the heat radiate up through the thin leather soles of her sandals.

She rounded a curve and the long stretch of Bombora beaches stretched out in front of her, the Cove's dated glass mansions twinkling on the northernmost point. The swell had dropped and only a few lanky, wetsuited figures were riding the gentle waves. On the rocks in front of Vaga more surfers reclined, glistening like seals with their wetsuits pulled down to their waists and the usual small tribe of bikinied young women crouching alongside them. Even from this distance she could recognise Guil, the cross of his legs and his dark curls already dried from the sun and brushing his shoulders. He was never one for large groups but Renata was relieved to see him looking relaxed, twisting left and right as he followed the lively conversation around him, the occasional loud laugh carrying on the wind to her as she descended the steps to the beach.

She decided to give him more time to enjoy his friends before coaxing him away and dipped into the relieving cool interior of Vaga. She ordered a coffee from a sweaty looking barista and indicated that she would sit at the front bar, facing the beach. She wanted a few more stolen moments observing her son. It was such a luxury to see him back here, fitting right back in with his old friends. He had barely been a teen when they had moved away, something that Renata still regretted. She knew there was no point in beating herself up for her decision at that time — who could have possibly predicted what would happen? — but the feelings of guilt still plagued her and no amount of reassurance from Guil could appease them. On days like this, however, with a light breeze caressing her shoulders and a sky as perfect and blue as a Portuguese dinner plate, she allowed herself to feel a deep gratitude.

From behind her, the barista leaned over to place her coffee on the wooden bar. She twisted around to thank his retreating figure, and as she did her eyes fell on two men having what looked like a tense conversation. One of them she recognised as the owner of Vaga, a large man with cheeks riddled with broken capillaries. He was talking to a much slimmer man, around the same age but in much better condition and wearing expensive looking leisure wear. They were sitting together at a table with paperwork spread in front of them. The owner held his massive hand in a fist which he kept lifting and letting fall onto the sheaf of papers, the table vibrating each time he did so. It was clear he was agitated. The well-dressed man appeared to be listening sympathetically, staring into an empty espresso cup. His eyes suddenly lifted and he caught Renata's gaze. For a moment they took each other in before Renata quickly swivelled and searched for Guil again.

Her son was now on his feet and pulling a t-shirt over his head, his wetsuit still draped around his hips. Renata blew into her coffee and hurriedly swallowed it one gulp. She was bending down to retrieve her wicker basket from the floor when a shadow fell across her from the beach side of the bar. The well-dressed man was now standing in front of her, an inquisitive frown marring his features.

"Nata?"

No one had called her that in years. It was the moniker she had lived with throughout her school years, the small children in her primary classes preferring a two-syllable version of her name out of laziness, not unkindness. All names were short-ened. Angela became Ang. Rebecca, Bec. Naomi, Nomi. And this man, she now realised, was Michael. Mick.

The two blinked at each other. Renata knew that this was bound to happen. It was just a matter of time before she would run into someone from her past.

"Wow, how are you? Haven't seen you for a while. Where have you been hiding?" Mick smiled broadly at her.

"Oh, I moved away for a while. Out west. I *really* missed the ocean." Over his shoulder she could see Guil gathering his belongings and bending down to grab his board. "I don't want to be rude, but I really want to catch my son before he heads off."

Mick twisted around and took in the group of surfers on the rocks.

"Ah! Which one is yours?"

"The one with long curly hair. Green and yellow board." Renata could not keep the pride from tinging her voice. Silhouetted against the ocean behind him, Guil's caramel skin was even darker and he had the enviable V-shaped torso of a regular surfer. At the age of seventeen, the awkward lankiness of his mid-teen years had given way to the broad shoulders and strong limbs of a young man.

Mick turned back to her.

"I have two kids as well, perhaps a bit older than your son there. They have both moved away to the city. The surf culture was nothing for them."

Renata nodded politely, but didn't say anything nor inquire for extra details, even though she knew this was the expectation.

Mick filled the silence. "He's still in school?"

Renata nodded. "He's doing his HSC this year."

"So, where are you living?"

"In one of the blocks along there," Renata lifted her chin to indicate the direction of the Esplanade.

"Which one?"

Mick saw Renata's face turn wary, a cloud passing across her features.

"The Palisade," she said hesitantly. She resented having to answer him, but could not think of a fictitious name fast enough.

Mick smiled broadly. "Know it well!"

Mick saw Renata's face close even more. She was now standing with her wicker basket hanging over one shoulder, waiting to be excused. A tiny, taut muscle twitched at the side of her mouth. Any curiosity she had shown at the beginning of their encounter — admittedly, not much — had completely dissipated. In fact, she now looked almost hostile.

"OK. Well. Have a good one, then." Mick stiffened in response to her behaviour. He stepped backwards and tilted forward from the hips in a self-conscious and awkward bow.

Renata nodded and ducked away without a word. She felt his eyes on her while she hurried over to her son, the bright yellow of her sundress flapping around her legs.

Nata. Memories flooded back of her primary school only a few streets away. The wet figs that fell from the trees and splattered the playground and attracted swarms of flies. Sitting cross legged on the netball court for morning assembly, the ground under her bare thighs already hot and leaving red dimples and tiny beads of gravel in her skin. She had not been overly popular, but she was a well-liked and accepted member of her class. She had had a handful of close friends who also came from Mediterranean families, and although they were not in any way ostracised, they preferred to keep to themselves. That way, they would not have to explain the strong smell of foods like bacalao in their homes when their friends came over to play, nor would anyone constantly ask, "What is your Mum *saying*? What language is *that*?"

Guil left his board in a rack by the surf lifesaving club before heading through the park towards the main street. Renata fell comfortably into step beside him.

"Who was that?"

"No one important, just someone from school." Renata did not mention hoping that she would never see him again. She could not explain her strange aversion to her old schoolmate, her desire to keep her life here in Bombora private and protected.

Mick, a few minutes behind them, was at the same time hoping he *would* see her again, which was not at all unlikely. She was, after all, one of his tenants.

. . . .

Late afternoon. The sun had peaked high above the centre of the peninsula and was now dropping down quickly behind the row of high-rises on their western sides, bringing welcome shade to the Esplanade for the first time all day. Shards of cool, dark shadow sliced up the pavement that Renata and Guil were following home to the Palisade. Renata revelled as she walked barefoot, swinging her sandals from one hand, several footfalls landing in a cool puddle of shade, the next few smarting as they landed on cement still burning with heat.

Renata nudged Guil. "There's my favourite house. See that lady out the front? I remember seeing her sitting there even before we moved away. I would come jogging along here in the morning and she would always be sitting out with her husband having tea and toast. It's not the fanciest house along here but it's always been my favourite. Such beautiful woodwork on the veranda, see? Federation style." It could also be that much of her affection had been directed towards the peaceful couple who had sat together in such companionable silence with their breakfast each morning. To think relationships could be so silent, and yet clearly so enduring. Renata could only imagine.

"Can't see her husband, though."

"She might be alone now. Nice for her, that she can stay here in her home. So she's managed to hold on. No one has bought her out. I bet the property developers have been circling like vultures. Good on her."

"A few of the guys I surf with are squatting in the house next to hers. They probably keep her up all night, poor thing. Funny music and funny smells."

"Squatting? In Bombora?"

"Yeah. You'd be surprised. Lots of the guys who have moved down from up north are either squatting or have negotiated really cheap rents. We're idiots to pay as much as we do, Mum. Rents are dropping. Fast. And some people aren't even bothering to pay at all anymore."

"I'm pretty sure if I didn't pay rent someone would be banging on our door pretty bloody quickly."

"I've heard a lot of landlords have moved away. They can't afford the upkeep on their properties with all the new environmental codes coming in, especially the ones so close to the coast. So they can't get landlord insurance but they can't sell either. Who would *buy* on the coast these days? So they just rent out for what they can get. The places are dumps, though. They're not investing anything into them anymore."

Renata made a sound of dismissive disbelief.

"No, really, Mum, even in our block. I'm out at night more than you, I can see all the empty windows when I'm coming home. I am pretty sure a couple of flats have squatters in them, too. They don't have electricity connected but they use camping gear to cook and candles for light. I see the flickering."

"But the security doors? How do they come and go?"

"These are the ground floor ones I am talking about. I guess they just climb over the balconies. Or maybe no one is collecting security keys when people leave and they just get passed around. Dunno."

This hit Renata hard. She was happily forking out what to her was a huge amount of money to live in what she thought was a high-security building. She loved the heavily spring-loaded door in the foyer that she needed to pull open with two hands. Nothing was more gratifying to her than the obnoxiously loud *bang* it made when it swung shut behind her at the end of the day. True, she was so focused on getting up to her apartment she barely clocked her neighbours. She didn't have a car so she never entered the car park; she never used the common storage areas on the ground floor, preferring to live with as few possessions as would fit within her own four walls. She didn't know or care about her neighbours but she assumed they were all of a certain calibre.

"Oh, that can't be right. I am going to speak to the real estate agent about that!"

"Do you even know who our landlord is?"

"No, I pay the agency. A lot. And now you're telling me I'm being ripped off and living in a … surfie commune!"

"Really, Mum, is it such a bad thing? They're good people, the ones I know anyway. Some have lost homes in the constant floods up north and they just want to hang out here and enjoy the waves. The surf down here is awesome now, we get sets that you used to have to travel up north for. Don't you think Bombora has become much more relaxed since we lived here before? It's more 'live and let live'."

Do they even work?" Renata had been raised by a family that valued hard work over everything else. Bombora had been largely built by tradesmen and labourers from Portugal, Spain, Italy, Malta, and Croatia, all leaving post-war Europe to find better lives in Australia. A whole tribe of them found Bombora, which — full of sweet pine-scented parks, rock pools and swooping packs of sea birds — reminded them of the best of the Europe they had left behind. Renata's father and uncle had been part of the exodus from Portugal, finding plenty of work laying foundations for homes, mixing cement at building sites, and, as their reputations grew and their English improved, supervising building crews on larger civil projects such as the Ringside Shopping Mall and the bridge at Lilyvale. Work was a privilege and a duty. Renata couldn't hide her contempt for people who did not work.

"Some don't work, although some would like to. More and more shops and cafes are closing so there is much less casual work available. That's why they're happy to squat for a while. Who knows how long this will last for?"

"How long *what* will last for?"

"The north has been practically decimated by storms and flooding. The good waves have moved south for now, but everyone expects eventually the bad weather will follow. It's started, you know that. I heard Vaga is closing. One of my mates is dating a waitress there. Lou has started to let people go. Heard he could not renew his insurance so can't take the risk of staying. He's not even sure if he'll get any money from the king tide damage he had a few weeks back."

Renata recalled Lou and Mick huddled over paperwork that very morning in Vaga. She had always had a soft spot for the place, and not just because she could drink coffee at the front bar and spy on her son. Her father and uncle had helped build it. It had been a quick job, Renata recalled. It was not a complicated building, just a square annex attached to the Complex next door. The bar in the centre, which housed the cash register and an expensive imported coffee machine from Italy, had been the hardest part. It was essentially a long concrete slab, but curved, then covered in the same iridescent tiles that had been chosen for the walls and floor. The whole room should shimmer as if encrusted with shell and coral, the work crew had been instructed, with the wave-shaped bar the centrepiece and the only curve in the otherwise square construction. The crew had struggled with that bar, she recalled, getting the arc smooth and creating the tapered end, as delicate as the whorl of a mermaid's tail. Yet they had pulled it off; her father had made sure of it. To honour the hard working Portuguese crew who had sweated through long, hot days to complete the beautiful and unique bar, Lou named the restaurant "Vaga" — short for "vaga de calor," meaning "heatwave" in their language.

"So, what are you saying? That eventually we will have to move on? Are we safe in the Palisade?"

"We are not as close to the coast as some of the high-rise blocks, so I think we're fine. For now. Personally I would not want to be living in The Glades or Sunrise. Those buildings are so old the concrete is crumbling off and the metal holding the balconies on is getting exposed to the salt in the air. Scary. One hectic king tide and I reckon they'll come right off and float away. Let's wait till that happens and then we'll know it's time to clear out."

Guil swatted his mother on her shoulder, trying to lighten her mood. He had not planned for the conversation to turn so dark. "Look, I don't think it's an emergency but we need to be realistic and read the signs. Climate change has already started to affect the lives of real people we know, Mum. My friends from up north, and … well, you know. What happened to him. That was fire, but still — it's all climate change, isn't it?"

Now Renata stopped dead in her tracks. Guil turned to face her. She was rigid, frozen in place. Only her sandals moved, swinging from a clenched fist.

"Sorry, I should not have mentioned him."

Renata slapped a hand over her mouth and shook her head. "No, no. We do have to talk about that day. Not now, but soon. We've been avoiding discussing it for so long. I can't sleep. I can't forget it. And I want to explain. But please. Not now."

"Deal. Let's go enjoy the sunset from our balcony, Ma. We are safe. I promise."

CHAPTER 4. MICK

Mick was woken early by cockatoos screaming at the sunrise. Sam had kicked off the bed covers and was breathing heavily, one shuddering breath in and a soft wheezing breath back out. Mick suspected she had stayed up much later than he had last night, finishing the bottles of white wine from the entertaining they had done over the weekend. Not for the first time, he pondered whether it was an issue he needed to confront. He took in her sleeping profile in the dim bedroom, her lips hanging open slackly and saliva pooling at one side of her mouth.

Ah, leave it, he thought. The kids are gone. She doesn't get violent. Her blood work keeps coming back clean (and he's tipped off their discrete general practitioner, who has been looking after the family for years).

"Well *I* feel good!" he told himself triumphantly. He had been avoiding alcohol for a few weeks now, had lost some weight, and was enjoying sleep of a depth and quality that surprised him. He checked his phone. 5:17 am.

"Up and at it!" He had fallen asleep last night with his AirPods in, listening to a productivity podcast that advised spending five minutes making a mental plan for the day before getting out of bed. The breath coming out of Sam, who had now swivelled towards him, was so rancid he decided to construct his list in the shower.

He stood under the prickling warm jets and began.

First, urgently find out what John's plans were. Not about moving (he couldn't care less about which Southern Highlands enclave would embrace John, Nat and their questionable tastes), but he urgently needed to know what John's intentions were about their significant portfolio of shared investments. Depending on what John told him, he might need to schedule an urgent meeting with his bank and lawyers.

Second, drop in on Rodney, the mayor of Bombora. He sat on a pile of money Mick himself had helped raise over the last few years for flood water protection projects for the peninsula. Rodney had been fobbing off Mick for months now. He would show up and demand to see the plans. Today. This morning. He wanted to see a schedule of meetings that would be needed to discuss alternatives and ratify decisions. This could not wait any longer. After spending Saturday morning with an irate Lou at Vaga he realised he had been too complacent. That would *not* continue.

(The thought of Saturday at Vaga invoked a sudden image of Renata. Yellow sundress, tanned shoulders, long legs and leather strappy sandals entwined around her lovely ankles. He intentionally blocked the reality of her cold reaction to him and pictured instead her eyes creasing with a flirtatious smile, her thick hair pooling in her collarbones. His penis made a half-hearted attempt to respond to these images, but even the warm water could not coax much more of a reaction out of him. He would need to get involved proactively if he really wanted to go down that path. But he was too far along on his productivity kick to allow himself those minutes by himself in the oversized grey slate shower, and the sound of Sam now lightly snoring was distracting. It could wait. Back to the list).

Third, drop into the real estate agent and get a rundown of exactly how many tenants he had, in which buildings, and the status of the leases. First and foremost, the Palisade.

Showered and shaved, he stood in the driveway and took in the tangerine streaked sky and felt the warm air embrace him. The sun had come out after a couple of days of erratic electrical storms and there was a tangible pulse of insects busy at work rebuilding their homes after the rain. And was that the sound of the surf he could hear? It was highly unusual to hear it from this side of the narrow peninsula, even this early in the morning. He decided that he needed a new number one item on his list: coffee at Vaga.

His car dipped down towards the beach. Normally the view of the beach from the vantage point as he crested the hill at this time of day was of a glistening, wide bowl. Sometimes it appeared so flat, the slant of the rising sun's rays gave the impression of a solid surface. You could almost believe ice-skaters would glide in and start whirling around each other. He had admired this view many times when he had brought Ethan and Adele down to the beach for pre-school swim squad.

Today, the ocean was a mass of churning foam, waves moving in all directions and being sucked back with visible force. Waves, not rolling in the usual orderly sets, collided with each other and sent white spray into the sky. There were no surfers in the water. After Mick had parked and walked the short distance to the Complex, he saw a few of them suited up and clustered on the rocks — the same rocks where Renata had met her son — holding their boards and staring into the sea.

Shouts came from the rock pool to the left of the beach. A small group of power-walkers had stopped and were leaning over the rails of the Esplanade, yelling down to a group of swimmers who, still dry, were huddled together at the edge of the pool holding their towels and goggles. Swimming this morning was not possible; the rock pool was like a Jacuzzi.

Mick spotted one of his friends who was rugged up in a plush tracksuit and was restraining a Jack Russell terrier tugging feverishly on its leash. "G'day mate. What's going on?"

"A baby shark got washed over the wall by a wave."

"How on earth can you see it in that churn?"

"It's in there mate, saw it myself. If you keep your eyes on the edges, you might see it. It's distressed and has been banging into the walls."

"Well, we'll have to wait till it calms down a bit and get it out of there. What do you think it is?"

"Ah, just a Port Jackson or wobbegong. Don't worry mate, it's not *Jaws*!"

Mick shuddered. He had always hated swimming in rock pools. As a child, he had been a part of the Bombora Nippers, a club for youth which met at the beach every Sunday morning to compete in races, either sprinting in the sand and diving for flags or taking part in relay races in the rock pool. Not only was it exhausting, but the kids needed to dodge blue bottles drifting in the water and avoid touching the cavities in the sides of the rock pool walls where blue ringed octopus were known to hide. The only good thing about being in the Nippers was his mother wrapping him in a warm towel at the end of the session and the hot chips he was allowed to buy afterwards from the milk bar.

"Where are the lifesavers?" asked Mick. "Isn't this their job?"

"The tower is empty. Guess they figure because the beach is closed they don't need to be here."

"Isn't that exactly when they should be here? There's always one dick who will decide to go for a swim, even in a swell like this."

Mick sighed. Despite his aversion to rock pools, it would be his job to get the damn baby shark out. He was Bombora's fixer, whether he liked it or not. Everyone came to him with their problems and he had an uncanny knack of wandering straight into problem situations like this one. Even now he could see a few faces in the small knot of onlookers staring at him with expectant eyes.

"I'm not really dressed for it. I'll come back with my swimmers when the tide has started to go back out. I won't be able to see it in this foam."

Two hours later and true to his word, Mick stood on the steps leading down into the rock pool, disgusted by the feeling of slimy seaweed under his toes. The crowd of onlookers leaning on the wooden rails behind him had expanded, all trying to catch a glimpse of the shark as it swum agitatedly in its unexpected enclosure. The waves had stopped pouring in from the eastern wall of the rock pool, but patches of foam still drifted about making it difficult to see below the surface. Mick waded in slowly, flinching as clusters of gelatinous, thick weed wrapped around his legs.

Not sure of how best to proceed, he kept wading until he was a metre or so away from the back wall, the salty water fizzing around the level of his navel. Assuming the shark must be trying to stay in the deeper water, he stood still and peered into the grey water. An excited cheer from the crowd behind him caused him to tense nervously and swivel his head, following their united gaze to the shiny patch of skin that broke the surface of the water behind him. He felt an underwater current tickle his legs as the shark descended and swam behind him. This happened several more times as Mick took a wide stance and curled his toes into the soft sand of the rock pool's floor. *It's just a matter of time before it swims in front of me*, he thought. *It's getting curious.*

The first time the baby shark swam in front of Mick he tensed, trying to scope out the size of it. Struggling to see into the murky water, he assessed it as being around half a metre in length. He remained in place, waiting for the shark to pivot at the southern wall and return. He assessed again his distance from the back wall and shuffled slightly forward. The shark had started to move with a regular, smooth tempo, back and forth, and seemed to be as equally keen to explore Mick's sudden presence and dimensions as Mick was about itself. The third or fourth time he swam between Mick and the back wall of the rock pool, Mick thrust himself forward with his full force. Grasping the wall's rough rock with his hands, he simultaneously pulled hard with his arms as he pressed his pelvis to the wall, feeling the muscular shark thrashing at the level of his hip bones. Mick knew he had only one chance, and pushed with the full force of his legs so as not to allow leeway for the shark to escape. Simultaneously, he reached down into the water and in one frantic movement, hefted the shark up and out of the water, depositing it onto the broad rim of the rock pool wall. It landed with a wet thud and Mick stared into its unblinking black eye as it immediately started to writhe. One push was all it needed to deposit the shark back into the open ocean.

A cheer erupted from the promenade behind him and Mick waded back out of the rock pool, still disgusted at the sensation of the shark's cold, sandpaper-textured skin. He had scratched his hands badly performing his panicked, scooping manoeuvre, salt water stinging his superficial wounds.

He muttered to himself as he accepted several back slaps and retrieved his towel and clothes. *Now can I start my day in peace?*

. . . .

Mick slouched into a dark kitchen, utterly depleted.

What a fucking day. His keys clattered onto the marble island and he gripped the edge with both hands, his head falling forward. He watched his own chest rise and fall. He could smell the residue of the long day clinging to him — soap, salt water from the rock pool and that goddamn slimy shark, sweat from the last couple of hours of meetings that careened from disappointing to outright shocking. His own breath reeked of stale coffee; he certainly had not had the time or the inclination to eat.

The day had started so well, so full of great intentions. He should have had that wank in the shower, he thought; maybe denying himself that pleasure this morning was the reason why he had been cursed with a day so baleful and malignant it verged on comical.

"*Hellooooo.*"

"Jesus!" he could not help but exclaim. "Sam, what are you doing sitting in the dark?"

"The sun went down and I just couldn't be arsed getting up."

Oh, this too, he thought. *Sam's pissed — again. She's in a fighting mood.*

He snapped the overhead light on. His wife blinked and turned her head away from him, taking only a moment to adjust to the illumination and resume her straight-backed posture, facing him with a dark expression. Legs crossed, festive dress, make-up like a circus clown who had been dunked in a barrel of water, smug smile. Fight in her eyes.

A half-full glass of white wine sat in front of her.

"Sooooooo. How was the day?"

He would be unable to make her understand even if she were sober.

"Oh Sam, will you please just go to bed?"

"But I am not tired. I have news. Do you have news for *me*?"

Where should he possibly start with his news? That John had indeed bailed on their investments, sending a pile of legal documents that gave Mick two choices; buy him out at a "fair" discount, or agree to a fire sale of their entire investment portfolio. John, of course, was not available to discuss any of this personally, leaving the whole nasty business to be executed by his lawyer — a new lawyer in the city whom Mick had never heard of. They had always shared the same legal team here in Bombora, but this apparently was worthy of fresh legal blood. Mick had spent a rushed thirty minutes on a video call with her; she, composed in her prim, high-necked white blouse with ridiculous pussybow and too much rouge, while he shouted and banged his desk and covered his computer screen with enraged spittle. She sat in front of a tasteful botanical etching and calmly stated the position of her client, as if he were a faceless enigma. This was John, *fuck it*, not "my client". This was the same man he had snorted cocaine with in the Cove multiple times. This was the man whose arse crack he had literally checked for ticks while on camping trips with their kids. Mick had been so angry bile rose in his throat.

The panicked calls to his bank and then his insurance broker that followed. The picture coming into obscene focus, like looking through a kaleidoscope and seeing all those undefined blobs suddenly converge, the snap of the image in front of your eyes. Once it's there, it's unwavering and unapologetically inert. Sharp-edged, undeniable.

He sighed. "Why don't you tell me *your* news?" *And then go the fuck to bed.*

"Two more families."

"What?"

"Two more families going, Mick. The McCallums. OK, I know you don't like them much but I became close to Jayne over the last year. She got up during that terrible storm we had a couple of weeks ago to check her dogs were inside and saw a bloody caravan floating past her jetty! And, get this, you won't believe it, the Jamiesons are going too!"

This did give Mick pause. The Jameisons were an entrenched Bombora family. Hedley's father had owned the old ballrooms, before they were pulled down and replaced with a food court and a bowling alley. Hedley had taken his inheritance and grown a restaurant empire, most recently branching into craft beers from a factory near Mick's own commercial storage units at Devlin Point.

"We can't wait any longer, Mick. We can at least recoup some of our losses if we move fast. Every day we wait, the market drops. I am sick of going out for a walk around the block and seeing the streets full of removal vans. We became rich being first movers. Ahead of the curve every time. We can't be laggards this time."

Mick's head was swimming.

"I know John has sent you an offer. I heard it's reasonable."

His head snapped up. "Do you know where John and Nat have gone? Do you know that fucker has screwed me over?"

"Did he screw you over, or has he been trying to talk sense to you for months?" Sam's bleary eyes narrowed. "You and your crazy idea of a sea wall. Are you serious? First, it's not bloody feasible, second, no one wants to enjoy a view of a seawall!

You and the ridiculous ideas you have been dumping up at the council! They laugh at you, Mick!"

Mick remembered that he had meant to catch up with the mayor, Rodney, today, but he'd been well and truly diverted from the game plan he had formulated this morning in the shower.

"I have raised so much money for that goddamned council! The least they could do is pick one of my ideas — *just one!* — and try to do something to protect the peninsula! I suppose Rodney Fuckface will be the next person you are going to tell me has scurried away!"

"It's a time bomb here. We are so vulnerable, sea on one side, bay on the other, one narrow bridge connecting us to the mainland. And it doesn't matter if the shit hits the fan next week, next month, or in five years. You know more than anyone that the market is king. It's all about tipping points. Enough people lose confidence and go, and this place becomes degraded and sad. We had it good here for so long, but it's over. We can at least afford to go and start again somewhere."

"You want to move to wherever John and Nat have gone? And the fucking Jamiesons? What, are they building some sort of posh commune in the hills somewhere? Bet the fuck wherever they go, they are displacing a whole lot of local people, building huge walls around themselves to keep them out. You've always loved the way wealth insulates you, haven't you?"

"Oh and you don't? When was the last time you hung out with all your tenants? You don't even know who they are. You only care that you get your fat cheque every month. They are faceless, nameless and uninteresting to you! You are no better than me!"

"So you are saying we should just go and abandon them to their fate? We grew up here! Your parents grew up here! How can you think of leaving so easily? What about your mother, in the home? Would you just leave her there? You can practically see the sand from her balcony."

"I'll take her with me."

"You'd rip your eighty-year-old mother out of that place and take her somewhere else? You're completely overreacting. Yes, the weather has been brutal lately but we need to adapt. We haven't even implemented any kind of measures yet. That fucking council, they need a boot in the arse. It's *their* job to be worrying about all this. And I'll make them."

"It's too late for all that! The kind of fixing this place needs, one of the most vulnerable suburbs on the coast, will take years. We left it too late. *You* left it too late."

"Me? *ME?*" Mick was so angry his eardrums felt like they were swelling, pulsing hotly. "Do you know what I am doing most days, while you are getting pissed at Vaga with the girls? I am the one visiting engineers, getting plans drawn up, taking them up to that complete waste-of-space Rodney. I actually think about how to protect this suburb all fucking day and all fucking night. What do you think about all day? When is a good time to switch from coffee to wine? Next holiday — Fiji or Tonga? Who to invite for dinner on Saturday?"

Mick drew breath. He was still gripping the marble benchtop. As angry as he was, and as sure as he was that Sam would remember little of this conversation when she woke — she would just have her characteristic, generalised fog of quiet shame after a night of drinking — he was shocked at the venom in his voice. *It's really come to this,* he thought. *This is how I speak to her now.* The realisation that, regardless of where they lived, they could no longer be together presented itself quietly in his mind, and his body responded with a relaxation so sudden he felt himself sway on his feet.

With the kitchen suddenly filled with silence, Sam burst into tears. "Don't you get it? We have no choice but to go! I am so tired of feeling like a climate refugee!" She slapped her flat hand on the counter, her thick gold rings chiming against the marble.

Disgusted, Mick went to bed.

CHAPTER 5. SAM

Sam dozed. She heard the whine of the fridge door opening and closing, the slam of the back door, the long moan of the garage door retracting, and the barely perceptible sound of the expensive engine of Mick's car as it deftly managed the incline of the driveway and disappeared down the street.

The anxiety was there, her trusty morning companion. It hovered behind her heavy eyelids, waiting patiently for her to wake fully and stoke it with disjointed memories from yesterday and last night. She fumbled with one hand under the covers to discover that she was still wearing yesterday's dress. She managed to lift her head and through blurry, crusted eyes saw a palette of colours smeared across her satin pillowcase. This wouldn't be the first time she had had to throw one away after being ruined by her makeup.

Aspirin was stored in a small lacquered box next to her side of the bed. She was no rookie. She squeezed a round pill from its plastic casing and crunched down on it, feeling the bitter shards scatter across her dry tongue. Her nerve endings felt thousands of times more perceptive this morning. She dreaded the walk down to the kitchen but needed some water. The plaster-like consistency in her mouth was making her gag.

She entered the kitchen, characteristically spotless. Her empty wine glass, smeared with lipstick, jumped out at her. This she found strange. Mick usually cleared the kitchen of all remnants of her drinking before he left, stashing glasses into the dishwasher and taking empty bottles to the recycling bin outside. Sam knew this was called "enabling behaviour" and although she had recognised it as such, she had always been grateful that she could start each day fresh, as illusory as it was.

She picked up the glass and fumes of warm Chardonnay rose to meet her. She knew that she and Mick had stepped over a precipice last night. Although she couldn't remember every word, she felt the truth of what had transpired settle into her exhausted body. They had always bickered, like most couples she knew, but last night signalled a new and undeniable reality. She could easily summon the feelings of contempt she had for him, even now. And the hatred — yes, hatred — he had for her had been clearly visible on his face.

As she looked down at herself in yesterday's clothes, she could not blame him. She had been drinking constantly since the children had moved out. Far from being teetotal while they were at home, she had at least managed her consumption so that she could (probably) jump into the car for any sudden emergency. She had it down to a fine art and knew her sweet spot was roughly half a bottle a night, at most three quarters. If she left at least one pour in the bottle, she could say to herself, "You are not on one bottle a night." She would start drinking during dinner preparation, sipping slowly, and then would give herself a nice top-up for the meal. Once she was fairly certain no one needed her for anything else, she would reward herself with one more generous pour after the kitchen was cleaned and the kids had retreated to their rooms. That was a moderate day. There were some days that she went much further.

Adele had moved out first, and Ethan followed the year after. Mick was constantly working and work spilled over into their social lives. There were friends and associates of Mick to entertain and he was constantly fundraising with Sam expected to do her part. They had the perfect home for entertaining. Mick started having wine and beer delivered directly to the house, the delivery men even stacking it into the three separate fridges and taking all the cardboard discretely away. It was like having the mini-bar in a hotel room miraculously replenished every day, except there was nothing mini about the fridges in Sam's home. Mick pressured Sam to socialise more with the wives of his business associates, and she found as time went on that she needed a quick shot of white wine before she even left the house. She would be expected to hold court, Mick's perfect little other half.

Sam perched on the same stool she had been slumped on the night before. She took in the clinical lines of her kitchen, white surfaces sparkling in the morning light. *You could perform surgery on this slab of marble*, she thought, stroking it. Cold. All of her expensive gadgets, the many sets of wine glasses, hidden away behind sleek cupboard doors that needed the most gentle nudge to spring open with a soft sigh. The humming fridge devoid of photos and community notices about bin pickups, just a polished silver hunk of metal vibrating coldly, as anonymous and discreet as a morgue door.

She visualised the kitchen that had once stood here, a phantom kitchen from the past emerging through the glossy showroom kitchen of the present. It had taken up roughly one quarter of the floor space. Brown cupboards, yellow Formica counters, orange and beige tiles on the wall. You could have a pot of Bolognese simmering and splattering all over the wall and you wouldn't see it, so garish were the colours back then. She smiled at the memory. Onions and garlic hung in a wire basket from the ceiling. The fridge, a shuddering old Westinghouse, was covered in notes that had been sent home from school and crayon renderings of farm animals, circuses and rocket ships, "FOR MUMMY" scrawled in large, shaky capital letters at the bottom. Sam could vividly see Adele and Ethan running in and out while she cooked, the screen door squeaking constantly and slamming behind their tanned little bodies. Sticky fingers covered in orange cordial leaving marks over walls, tiny hands reaching up for bowls of grapes and plates of vegemite sandwiches to take out and eat on the grass.

She swivelled around on her stool and took in the huge entertaining area. This used to be their massive backyard with a large frangipani tree raining blossoms down on them all summer long. Now, the entertaining area flowed through to the semi-enclosed deck, with wide cement steps leading down to a sparkling swimming pool that ran almost to the edge of their property. The jetty and boatshed were the only remnants that remained of the old garden. Barely a scrap of grass had survived. There was so much cement reflecting the sun's rays that Sam needed sunglasses just to walk outside, even without her daily hangover.

She felt a surge of remorse. She could picture herself standing in her old kitchen, looking out through the old bevelled glass windows that needed to be wound back with a small handle, watching her children on the grass. In summer, she would put the sprinkler on and let them run through it for hours, clad in their thin cotton underpants.

Her cheeks flushed with anger. Why had they built over the garden? Why did they need to create so much entertaining space? Between the two huge Italian sofas facing each other in the living room, the dining table for twelve, the outdoor area which could easily seat another eight people, she realised she could comfortably entertain forty people in this space. She could not even name forty people that she liked.

I was happy then.

This realisation broke through her simmering hangover and she winced, pressing the puffy pillow of skin between her permanently worried eyebrows. She allowed the memories to wash over her, both beautiful in the feelings they stirred up, but in equal parts terrifying in their distance from her now. She had taken so much pleasure in the evening meal routine, waiting impatiently to hear Mick's Toyota roll up on the grass and his car door slamming heavily. On hot evenings they had eaten on a picnic rug outside in the shade, then dining alcove next to the kitchen too hot to bear with its shag carpet and tiny windows. Mick and Sam would let the children run off as soon as they had eaten, and had held hands while they watched them paddle at the edge of the bay as it lapped at the sand beneath their stone wall. Their house was a simple red-brick bungalow, typical of that era, but they had secured an exceptional block of land. Sam, at the time, had thought the ultimate luxury was to be able to build a pergola in the garden so that they could eat *al fresco* at a proper table, not on a picnic rug. Mick had bought a huge round wooden table with a rotating "lazy Susan" at the centre, and she had loved having her parents over for meals, filling the table with fresh salads and simple barbequed fare. An Esky, filled with ice from bags bought at the service station, would be dragged out to the grass and studded with bottles of beer and soft drinks. Sam hung baskets of petunia and fuchsia from the corners of the pergola which dropped colourful tendrils that swayed in the breeze, blooming curtains that allowed the occasional glimpse of the glistening bay only a few metres away.

She could never have imagined the sleek, sprawling home that would replace all of that, all cool white stone and unobtrusive colours in so many shades of off-white her head spun; mushroom, ecru, Bavarian cream, dove wing, oyster, sea pearl. It all looked like varying shades of porridge to her now. She had never, in all honesty, even asked for it. Mick had insisted that with the way property prices were rising, the renovations would pay for themselves many times over. She had let herself be convinced, and so a whole team of architects and interior designers descended on her and stunned her with their glossy plans and illustrations, and they had had to move in with Mick's parents for eight long months while a new home was built up around the tiny red brick foundation. When they had finally moved back in, the sprawling expanse that was now her home numbed her with its neutral colour palette and she lost herself in the myriad of details that came hand-in-hand with all the extra rooms, nooks and crannies that needed to be filled and managed. She had to learn how to check and maintain the water in the outdoor Jacuzzi and to use the pool filtration system, and she needed to manage a small team of cleaners, gardeners, and tradesmen who were constantly installing or upgrading something. She was terrified of the high-tech security system they now had, sure she would punch a code incorrectly and unleash their shrill, wailing alarms onto the unsuspecting neighbours.

Why did he build me a palace, only to leave me all alone in it?

She caught a glimpse of herself in the Miele wall oven. Even in its inky black surface she could make out her dishevelled hair and bloated face. She picked up the dirty wine glass and threw it at her reflection. She left the shards of glass lying on the floor and went to get ready.

She needed to speak to her mother.

. . . .

Cafe Arrifana was tucked against the northern side of the North Bombora surf club in a bright room lined with jalousie windows. A few remote workers with lazy postures and exposed gluteal clefts were perched on a long bench sporting headphones and tapping furiously on their laptops. A smattering of small square tables filled the rest of the space. Most people were in their activewear, from three young women with messy ponytails and singlet tops (one of which was emblazoned with the motto "No Weights, No Dates"), to a table of impressively toned fifty somethings who had clearly just gotten back from power walking along the Esplanade. Their calves were ropey and covered with oversized, terracotta-coloured freckles and they all still wore caps pulled down over sweaty hair. An exhausted looking black poodle peered out from under one of the seats next to its own little silver bowl of water. The sound of the pounding waves beyond the back deck could be heard clearly, if not seen, and the smell of salt and seaweed filled the room.

"Right, Mum, what are you having?" Sam held a clipboard containing the menu in front of her face and started to read. "Eggs. You can have them poached with bechamel and smoked salmon. Scrambled comes two ways — Turkish, with harissa and a side of pickled beets, or truffled with gouda. Or you can ..."

"Oh my god, can I just have a plain old boiled egg?"

"I am sure they can do that. Toast? They have raisin, sour-dough, or activated linseed. Oh my god, you are right. When did things get so pretentious? Let's not even start on the coffee options."

A waitress bounded over in a crisp apron over her cut-offs and looked physically pained when Sam ordered simple boiled eggs and toast. "Do you have normal white bread? No? OK, sour-dough is fine."

"To drink?"

"Black tea with a side of milk for Mum, I'll take an oat flat white." Sam passed the clipboard back to the waitress who snatched it away as if such an innovative menu was wasted on these ungrateful women.

"I have to say the food at the nursing home is better than this."

"Well, maybe better for you Mum. But this seems to be what people like these days. Look at the women over there with the dog. They have acai porridge bowls served in half coconuts."

"Ridiculous. Nothing better than a tea and some hot Weet Bix. Why do people spend so much money on breakfast anyway? Dinner, I can understand. But brekkie? It should be a matter of shoving something in to kick start the day, no need to make such a production of it. I hardly ever ate breakfast anyway."

"You're not going to say something like, 'If the young people of today ate less avocado toast they would be able to afford a deposit for their first home' are you? Which dickhead prime minister said that?" Barb giggled and Sam's heart melted. She loved the easy banter she had always had with her tough, no-nonsense mother.

"So Mum, speaking of real estate. I wanted to actually talk to you about something."

Barb heard the tension in her daughter's voice. Both women fell silent while the waitress set their drinks down in front of them.

"I'm not sure how much you discuss this in the home, but you know, I've been thinking a lot about what's been happening here with the weather and you know I …"

"Climate change? Of course we discuss it in the home. What do you think we do? Sit around drooling at each other and comparing bowel movements?"

"Sorry, Mum, of course you discuss it. I wasn't sure how much you've been following it, to be honest."

"We are the ones who can really tell you how much has changed. Lizzie's granddaughter dropped in the other day and brought photos of the coastline where Liz had grown up, at Cape Levin. Liz was shocked at how much of the coast line has disappeared. The beach there used to be so wide you could get a horse going at a good canter along it. Now there is barely enough space to lay a towel. When the tide comes in, so much water surges up onto the beach you can become stranded in a matter of minutes. You can't take your kids down when the tide is turning anymore. It's too dangerous."

"Well good. So I can tell you what I need to tell you and I hope you understand."

"You're leaving."

As usual, conversations with her mother moved at a faster pace than she expected. She had prepared a much more detailed lead-in to her news, but Barb — as usual — just wanted the simple, unfancy version.

"OK, so when? To where? And is Mick going with you?"

Sam sighed. Of course her mother *also* knew the only sticking point in all this would be Mick.

"Mick has not committed to come with me and the kids are doing their own thing, as you know. I have a few irons in the fire and I don't have anything definite to tell you, I just wanted to ask you if you want to come with me."

"First, you throw me into a home and now I can come out? Because the water levels are rising?"

"There are reasons we needed to take you to The Pines, and to be honest, I would be looking for another place for you closer to wherever I end up. I just need to know if it's one of the things I need to factor in before I go too much further in my search."

Barb took her time tipping a little milk into her cup and slowly stirring.

"Maybe it's because I am in that home that I find it easier and easier to sink into the past. We have all those posters of Bombora on the walls, as you know. Pictures of all of the places that have been and gone that meant so much to me. The little bistro at Grace Brothers that always smelled of steamed milk and where you could get salmon sandwiches with the crusts cut off. The waitresses wore those frilly aprons, I guess 'Parisian' was the look they were going for. That was my fancy treat for the week, always after the Saturday morning shopping. It closed when you were still small but you would beg to come with me. You were so tiny in that leather booth!"

"I remember. You ordered for me once, and I thought you had said 'Egon Toast' to the waitress. I thought that was the name of the dish, that 'Egon' was a person or a place, something or someone fancy, it made me sit up straighter. Thought I was in for a real treat. But I had just misheard you; of course, you were just saying 'egg on toast'. I remember feeling disappointed when it arrived. Just bloody eggs." Sam felt a rush of affection for that little girl, full of anticipation for an exotic dish her mother had ordered for her.

Barb chuckled. "And then there was the milk bar down near the beach. No smoothies and that acai nonsense. Just plain old vanilla, chocolate or strawberry milkshakes in those huge metal cups. No one blinked if you ordered one for breakfast although they were filled with ice-cream. You could see the condensation rising up the sides and you kids would slurp so fast that you got brain freeze and would howl at me in pain and laughter."

"Picnics at the rock pool, Carols by Candlelight in the park, hot chips wrapped in newspaper. Sam, *all* of my memories come from this place. I haven't travelled. I have only seen your photos from Europe, the States, and the South Pacific. And believe me when I say I was *never* jealous. This is my home. I'd rather be taken away by waves than pick up and go somewhere else now. It would be a fitting end to be swallowed up by the same ocean I have seen and smelled every day for most of my life."

Barb gave a decisive tap of her tea spoon on the side of her cup for emphasis.

"But I will be asking the home to swap my bed out for an air mattress!"

And with that, Sam knew she could leave with her mother's blessing.

CHAPTER 6. OUT WEST

When they had first moved inland, Renata had tried to make the most of it. "We'll plant trees, a vegetable garden!" she told Guil. "You'll have to help." But coaxing Guil, then thirteen, outside to weed and water rows of cucumber, tomato and snake beans was near impossible. He was a helpful and calm child by nature, but the throbbing heat combined with mean horseflies kept him inside with excuses of homework. Renata would un-snake the dark green hose alone and drench her plants, watching the water disappear into the dry ground, never filling the cracks in the earth but leaving them wider and more desperate looking, yowling mouths screaming at her endlessly for water.

She watered morning and evening until the water restrictions came in and she watched as the plants shrivelled and drooped on the ground. They had never yielded much fruit. Nonetheless she had loved the ritual of twice-a-day watering, slowly shuffling past each plant, fondling the tiny hairy blossoms where miraculously a vegetable might sprout. Lizards took refuge in the shade of her stout tomato bushes and had scampered by her toes when she swept the hose over them, releasing shimmering arcs of droplets that cascaded down through the foliage and plopped onto the dirt. A completely white spider (she never knew there was such a thing), delicate and transparent in the morning slanted rays of sunlight, greeted her for two weeks from under the same crinkly leaf of a cucumber plant and then disappeared. Her sadness at its sudden absence was a stark reminder of her loneliness. She barely saw anyone other than Guil. And *him*, no matter how much she tried to avoid him.

When only the sturdy rosemary bushes remained with some semblance of life, she gave up on her garden. Now she had no excuse to be alone for those almost two hours a day outside. Most importantly, she lost her position of surveillance; her vegetable patch was on slightly elevated ground behind the house and had been the perfect spot to quietly check his comings and goings, the car slinking into the driveway or slinking out. All the while she appeared to be deeply absorbed in her plants, she had had a carefully trained ear out for him. It was especially invaluable in the evenings. Her radar was by then so finely tuned that the mere tone of his car door slamming, or how far back the front screen door was swung and with which velocity, could spur her into action. She would be inside in a flash, grabbing Guil from his desk — *"Come on, come for a little walk with me"* — and the two would disappear into the darkening evening through the back door. Guil knew to drop everything and follow his mother, even if he was working on the closing paragraph of an essay or about to nail an algebraic equation.

Sometimes they would hear him yelling as they tiptoed around the back of the garage and out onto the street, but more often than not, if he found a plate of food under a sheet of tin foil on the kitchen counter, the yelling would subside quickly. This put Renata in the almost comical position of thinking up new and interesting meals to leave out night after night in order to subdue and distract her intoxicated husband. Luckily she had a rich tradition of Portuguese cuisine to draw on and much of her daytime was spent devising, shopping for, and executing her culinary plans. When she and Guil would come back, the dark fully settled over their dusty street, the plate would be scraped clean, the tin foil in a ball on the counter, and loud, racking snores would be coming from the bedroom.

There were some surprising stretches of time — days, not weeks — when he would come home sheepish and relatively sober in time to eat with Renata and Guil. The three of them would sit awkwardly at the outdoor table swatting flies while they ate; Renata remaining vigilant for any rapid change in mood or facial expression that might cause her to hurriedly clear plates or suggest Guil help her with a chore in the garden. Guil spent these dinners leaning heavily onto one forearm and slouching over his plate even though his mother was pedantic about table manners. Talk was banal and excruciating.

"How's school?"

"Fine."

"Any exams coming up?"

"Nup."

"Swim race this Saturday?"

"Nah, season's over. We're just training."

Rarely did he try to engage Renata in conversation, but his eyes always sought her out. She stared at her plate and at each forkful of food as she carried it to her mouth, eating much faster than she usually would, and sprung up from the table to clean the kitchen as soon as her plate was clean. From her position inside at the sink she could theatrically demonstrate how busy she was with the loud bang and clatter of pots and pans and still keep an eye on her husband and son seated at the table outside through the little window.

It was always a good night when, after eating, he would announce he was going to visit his parents or brother who lived a short walk away. They were the reason they had moved out here in the first place, after his PTSD diagnosis and when it became clear that he would struggle to hold down full-time work. His parents had promised to help, reassuring Renata that it made sense for her small family to leave Bombora and move out to be near them in the west, even though leaving the ocean ripped her heart in two. Renata, the child of immigrants who had left the Atlantic coast of Portugal, herself now being forced to leave the Pacific coast of New South Wales, had the rhythm and pulse of the ocean in her veins, its daily ebb and flow in her blood. The morning they packed up their Subaru and hit the highway that would take them west counted as one of the saddest of her life. She had sat silently in the front seat and mentally bade farewell to two oceans and the two parents who had passed away and were buried next to each other in the cemetery they were now driving past on the way out west. As they drove, she watched the temperature slowly tick up on the car display and she felt herself harden, as hard as the ground flying by in a blur outside the window.

Renata had met her husband while working as a radio dispatcher for the State Emergency Services. Her desk had been next to the staff room and he would pass by multiple times a day, filling and refilling his battered green drink bottle just to have an excuse to stop and chat with her, which conversely meant he needed the men's room, on the other side of Renata's desk, just as frequently. On quiet days with few call-outs, he would pull up a chair to her desk and they would compare childhoods, he never having been out of Australia and genuinely intrigued by Renata's memories of growing up outside Lisbon. Renata had always found Australians impatient and a little outraged to hear about beaches in other countries — "*We* have the best beaches!" — but he happily listened to anything she had to say, including hearing about the many subtle ways in which beach life in Portugal was different to Australia; the colours of the rocks, the etiquette of towels and sunbeds, and the snacks you could buy from cafes and beach shacks. He was adamant he would travel to surf the massive wave at Praia do Norte beach in Nazaré when she told him it would often swell to twenty-five metres high.

It wasn't long before he was coaxing her out for coffees and then fully-fledged dates; he was the quintessential Aussie bloke, filling out his neat navy uniform with his broad surfer's shoulders. Her parents, who had always been overly deferential to authority figures in the way only immigrants can be, also loved him in uniform, black leather glistening at his waist and on his spit-and-polished boots, his breast pocket stamped with the colourful insignia of the Emergency Services. The fact that his work was physically demanding and often left him exhausted for days earned him extra respect from Renata's father, whose own lean body was riddled with the scars of decades of building work and who had nothing but contempt for men who earned their livings wearing starched shirts and smelling like talc, sliding around bland offices on their swivel chairs.

Even after they married (of course Renata's father solemnly gave consent) and Guil arrived on the scene, Renata got no sympathy from her parents for the fact that she often felt like a single mother.

"He's never here. He's either at work or at the pub calming down from work."

"Be grateful he has a job."

"You can't come over for dinner after all, he's been passed out in the bedroom all day and I don't think he's getting up."

"No worries, Renata, you bring the *bebê* over here. Let him sleep. He works so hard for you!"

And so it continued throughout Guil's early school years, Renata managing to create some semblance of a family life for her son by constantly recruiting her parents' help. Guil spent the afternoons after school at his grandparents' home so that Renata could keep her job as a radio dispatcher and there was always a meal waiting for her when she came to pick him up. The small apartment she shared with her husband became a place simply to sleep and change clothes. At her mother's insistence, she made an effort to make sure the fridge was well stocked although she knew that he mostly grabbed snacks on the road. There were times when he had an extended break from work that he would fall into hers and Guil's routine — sleeping nights, being awake for the whole day, and having enough energy for excursions during sunlight hours. Renata would watch him swing Guil up onto his broad shoulders and wade into one of the Bombora rock pools and her resentment would ease. She couldn't help but be proud of his thick chest and strong arms as he dipped Guil's little body into the shallow water and then threw him squealing into the air. He could balance his child on one bicep effortlessly as he strode out of the rock pool towards Renata, who would have a picnic waiting for them of chicken sandwiches and coleslaw. On days such as these, she did not hate being married.

Renata was not at work the day he was called out on the job that would change everything. She was not the one who received the call about a young man who had apparently jumped from the cliffs at the Gap, launching himself into a brutal westerly wind that was sending a sputtering tower of salt spray into the sky. All that Renata knew of what transpired next was what she read in reports or was told by the other members of the rescue crew that had been dispatched that day. Her husband never breathed a word of what had happened — at least not to her.

The one witness who had been there and who had then made the call to the Emergency Services described seeing the man simply step into what looked like a white, wet cloud that consumed him in a second — tracksuit, running shoes, bright orange beanie. *Gone in an instant*, she had said, bewildered, the only sound the impatient wind and the muffled sound of waves crashing on the rocks far below. At first she had not been able to ascertain whether he had in fact been right at the cliff edge, perhaps the spray-filled sky had given the illusion of him falling when he might have simply jumped down onto a rock ledge that she could not see? However, she only needed to take a few steps from her position a little south from where he had last stood to confirm that the cliff face was sheer. Anyone who went over it, accidentally or otherwise, was going all the way down.

The Emergency Services team arrived on the scene and found the witness in a local cafe, cocooned in a blanket that the proprietor had kindly draped over her. She held a trembling Cocker Spaniel in her lap, its dark brown eyes looking anxious over its damp and dripping nose. The woman, unlike her dog, was calm and walked with the crew towards the spot she had last seen the man, although she hung more than twenty metres back and cradled the small dog rather than walk too close to the edge. She would have watched the crew huddle and discuss matters. They would have quickly taken in the conditions — the wind, weather and tide — in order to come up with a plan. The strong wind would have made the option of using a helicopter near impossible, and the crew had used binoculars to confirm that this was not a life-saving mission, but rather a compassionate and very necessary clean-up duty, meaning no one would sign off on the higher risk of using a chopper. One of them would need to be winched down with a stretcher.

The paperwork refers to someone jogging back and informing the woman she was free to go, in fact, she was required to go. She would have been thanked; to have such a witness point out the exact location of the incident would have saved both the time and nerves of the rescue crew. A cordon was then erected around the area and at that point one of the crew reversed the rescue van over the grass to a position approximately five metres from the edge. The team quickly set up the winch and when it came to deciding which of them would be lowered down, Renata was not at all surprised that it was her husband who was selected. He would have undoubtedly volunteered; she knew him well enough to be sure of it. She could imagine the collective thinking of the crew, not really requiring much of a discussion to arrive at a rapid consensus. His upper body strength would be critical, being required to work quickly in a swinging harness against an unfavourable wind before the tide turned and the waves started pummelling in with more force. His years of surfing gave him an amazing core stability which would be helpful when stabilising a suspended stretcher with one arm, while leaving one arm free to push himself repeatedly back away from the cliff face.

The paperwork confirms he was lowered down at 11:18 am.

From this point on the report became very factual and brief, as the details could only have been provided by himself and the observations of the crew from above, whose visibility was greatly limited by the distance and flying sea foam. What Renata could glean is this: the operation went quickly and well at first, despite the jagged rocks preventing him from gaining a stable foothold from which to work. Anyone who works in this field knows full well how gruesome a high impact fall can be. The human remains may have been spread out over a relatively wide area, and Renata knew her husband would have taken the task very seriously, gathering as much as possible in his gloved hands and tucking it all into the exposed body cavity to be winched back over the top of the cliff. He even retrieved the orange beanie which had been flung farthest from the body. He would have been thinking of the family and of how important it would be for them to know as much was gathered from the rocks as possible in order to be able to bury or cremate. No one wants to imagine the tissue of their loved one being sucked into the sea to feed the fish or simply disintegrate into the salty brine.

From all accounts he was able to complete the task of packaging up the remains and strapping them to the stretcher, swinging like a pendulum from above, relatively quickly. But on the way up, when he would no doubt have been relieved the worst was over, the motor of the winch failed and he was left dangling. Not for ten or fifteen minutes, but for an entire sixty-seven minutes.

He never spoke about what went through his head in those long minutes, hanging halfway up a cliff face with a man who had been broken open on rocks and bundled back together and zipped into a body bag. The wind howled around them. The tide turned and the waves surged with even more power below his dangling feet. He had a radio receiver strapped to his belt but he did not use it; he probably could hear muffled cries from the crew above but they reported he simply hung in his harness, his head resting against the fist that gripped the cable. He was as still as his deceased companion.

And he was never the same again.

CHAPTER 7. THE BATHS

Renata pushed through a crowd of barefoot surfers clutching dripping kebabs outside the takeaway shop in order to access the narrow entrance to her real estate agency. The air conditioning blasted her face as she pushed open the heavy glass door and she heard the tinny jangle of a bell in an obscured back office. A door sprang open and a ruddy faced young man in a tight-fitting grey suit appeared, head cocked cheekily and holding his arms wide as if he intended to pull Renata into a hug. He reminded Renata of those maniacally cheerful wooden clown heads at Luna Park, the ones you shoved white balls into as they swung shudderingly from side to side. The name plaque on the office door spelled "RHYS WHITTAKER" in bold lettering.

"Well, hi!" His excessive enthusiasm made Renata wonder if she knew him, although he was much younger than herself and any of her old cohort from school. He was also not young enough to be one of Guil's friends, and his physique and pallid skin, which spoke of long hours on his backside in this air-conditioned cocoon, made him an unlikely candidate to be a surfer.

"Hi, I'm renting at the Palisade and well … just had some questions, really, about the building and the … ummm … other tenants …" She trailed off, realising that she might be crossing a line and potentially sounded a little like a stalker.

"Well, aren't you in luck!"

"Excuse me?"

"The owner of the Palisade just happens to be right here!"

With a theatrical sweep of an arm and wide grin, now resembling a circus ringmaster (he was just missing the top hat and whip), he flung open his office door to reveal Mick sitting cross-legged in a narrow visitor's chair, twisting around to look at her. He was dressed in his customary expensive leisure wear.

"Oh no, really, I can come back, I did not want to disturb your meeting ..." Renata could see sheafs of paper spread in front of Mick and a tower of manila envelopes stacked next to him. The way his face lit up when he saw her and seeing him scramble to push himself up from his chair charged her with anxiety.

"Of course not! Whatever questions you have about the building, you can hear it directly from the horse's mouth!" Rhys laughed, a high-pitched hee-haw to match his words, poking Mick aggressively in the shoulder. "Ha! Meet Mick — the horse! Ha, ha!"

Mick was now standing shoulder to shoulder with the boisterous agent, regarding her quietly.

"Of course, any questions about the tenants I could not possibly share with you," Rhys winked lewdly, using a mock-serious voice. "That could lose me my licence!" He erupted into laughter and grabbed Mick in a playful neck hold. "Mate, can you imagine ..."

With a slight eyeroll, Mick shook off the hand cupping his neck and pushed past Rhys, moving towards a small sofa in the entrance.

"Sit down," he encouraged Renata softly. "I can tell you about the Palisade, what I know anyway. We were actually just going through some paperwork on maintenance protocols now." His soft, steady voice was a mere whisper compared to Rhys's theatrical booming.

Renata was mortified. She had only wanted to come in and ask a few questions to put her mind at ease. Ever since Guil had spoken of squatters and sets of duplicate keys flowing through their hands she had not been able to relax. Now she was sitting on the world's tiniest corner suite under fluorescent lighting, knees almost grazing Mick's, face to face again with this man from her past who stared at her so attentively with watery blue eyes. The air conditioning continued to blast on her bare shoulders and a crop of goosebumps erupted down both arms. She hugged herself until she noticed how it lifted and presented her cleavage towards Mick, sitting too close for comfort. She released her arms quickly and sat on her hands.

"What would you like to know?"

"I ... I really would like reassurance that the security is being taken seriously. It's one of the reasons I rented that apartment. My son — Guil, you met him — he tells me Bombora is filling up with squatters. Apparently, a lot of people are leaving, landlords are abandoning their properties. He says a couple of the ground floor units in the Palisade might even have squatters."

Mick sat up straighter. This was news to him. Although he and John had developed the Palisade and kept a large share of apartments for themselves, they had sold off a handful on the lower floors. For all he knew, they might have changed hands over the years although he had no oversight of who the current owners were. John had always been more hands-on with the details of the rental properties they owned together, and now that he had disappeared from Bombora, Mick was left with the onerous task of forensically going through bulging manila folders with Rhys. It was hell.

"That doesn't sound right, but I can definitely look into it for you. If we do discover there has been some kind of breach, we'll deal with it. It's not ideal to have to replace the security lock and all the keys but it's doable."

"So it's true? Is squatting becoming a problem in Bombora?"

Mick could hear Sam's nagging in his head, snippets of their last fights before she left. Her "good" friends leaving and the "bad people" moving in was a constant theme. Mick, in his utter exhaustion and frustration with her, had discounted most of what she had said but now he pondered how true it might actually be. John was the last person he thought would ever evacuate and seek to minimise his losses, and yet he had. He can't have been the only one.

"I have heard of some people who have gotten nervous about the terrible year or two of weather we have had and left quickly." *Some people like my former best friend and business partner. Some people like my wife.* "What they don't know is that there are solid plans to protect the peninsula, many in fact that I am personally spearheading." Mick groaned internally but kept his face neutral. *Fuckface Rodney.* Renata did not need to know about the total incompetence of the local government. She was looking for solace, and he planned to provide it.

"I'm not going anywhere," he continued, "and you have my promise that I'll find out what's happening in the Palisade. It's in my best interest to do that anyway, right?"

Renata shrugged lightly, accepting his assurances with a curt nod.

Mick rubbed his eyes, and Renata noticed that he seemed thoroughly exhausted. He looked like he had aged ten years since the first time she had seen him in Vaga.

Her mothering instinct kicked in. "You look like you could do with some fresh air. It's like a fridge in here; I think you need to get outside for a while."

"Care to join me? I was actually going to head down to the old baths and have a coffee." He hadn't planned on that at all.

Renata paused before she answered. Although her default position was a clear no, she had to admit he had been very responsive to her concerns, and she had a raft of other questions she wanted to ask about the Palisade. Guil had terrified her with stories of flooded elevator shafts and crumbling balconies.

"Sure, I'd like that. I haven't been down there since we moved back here. I spent most of my childhood at those baths."

Mick could not believe she had said yes. He sprung up, keen to move before she reconsidered.

"Be back later, Rhys!" he yelled through the closed office door. They both heard the agent hefting himself up out of his chair, the springs of his swivel chair moaning. Mick hurriedly ushered Renata into the street before Rhys could scramble to get his office door open.

. . . .

Mick bought two flat whites from the kiosk and they ambled down the long side of the wooden baths, a sun-bleached runway of wood that jutted out into the calm bay. At the end, it turned around on itself three times to form a twenty-five-metre-long swimming enclosure. The entire structure looked like a large capital "P" hovering between two to four metres over the water level depending on the tide. As it was mid-week there were no lane markers out and the handful of latex-capped senior citizens languidly breast-stroking needed to keep a careful eye on each other so as not to collide. The lane markers, ropes with bright blue bobbing balls, only came out on Saturday mornings when the local swim clubs met up here for swim races, loud affairs with a starting pistol and throngs of spectators cheering the swimmers on.

Mick and Renata sat on the edge of the walkway, legs dangling, facing the white bobbing pontoon with starter's blocks marked with the numbers one to six in large black type.

"I did swimming training three times a week, and as if that wasn't enough, Mum brought me here every Saturday morning for the races." Renata smiled as she sipped her coffee. "I loved it though, especially the relays."

"Which was your best stroke?"

"I was fastest at breaststroke, but I liked doing backstroke the most because I liked watching people's faces looking down on me and cheering me on." Renata remembers how she would stretch her arms backwards and kick as hard as she could, the whole time looking out for her mother's proud face above. "One morning we came down and didn't realise it was the end of season carnival. Every other Saturday had been just as loud and crowded as this particular one. I swam my usual races — around six or so — and the minute I was done, Mum hurried me off to help her do shopping or some other errand. She had also completely missed that there was going to be a presentation and trophies would be handed out. She never really let on, but she understood very little English especially when it was so loud. So we left, and when I arrived at school on Monday, my teacher — whose kids were also competing — handed me a pillowcase filled with six trophies! I had won a place in every single race, but hadn't been there to collect them. I felt like such an idiot."

"You should have just felt proud, winning all those trophies."

"Yes, but when you are an immigrant kid, every single time you miss what to everyone else is obvious, you feel so exposed. Who comes to the final carnival, swims their heart out, wins, and then leaves? I was devastated that six times my name would have been called — probably mispronounced, by the way — and I would have been a no-show on the podium. I was so mad at Mum."

"What was your surname?"

"Nogueira. People here always say *Noggy-erra*."

"But that's not your surname now?"

Renata knew that eventually Mick would start digging about her romantic status, but she had to admit this was a smooth segue. "No, I still have my married name. Lincoln. Renata Lincoln. Everyone can pronounce that, thank God."

"Still? You mean, you …"

"My husband, Dean, died in those bushfires before Christmas last year. The ones out west. I was lucky to get myself and Guil out, but … Dean didn't make it."

"Oh my god, Renata, I am so …"

"Please, no one ever knows what to say. I don't know what to say about it either. It was hell living out there in general. I never wanted to go, and then for that whole summer the fires started circling and popping up closer and closer to us. It was always so hot, and some days you couldn't even go outside. On the day we had to evacuate, I had been at the local pool with Guil — he is quite a swimmer, too — and black ash was raining down into the water. We had all gotten so used to it, though — the smoke burning your eyes all the time, the hazy sky. I was so shocked to come home and see the fire crew in our street, telling us we needed to get out. I had no time to think, just ran inside and grabbed some stuff. Dean wasn't there. I assumed he was at his parents' place. They lived in the next street over. It's why we had moved out there in the first place. He spent more time there than at home."

"And? Was he there?"

"As it turned out, they found Dean's remains in our house afterwards. He must have been asleep on the sofa out the back. If he had been in our bedroom, I would have seen him. I obviously went in there to get some of my things. I didn't go out the back."

"How could he have slept through all that? The smell, the noise? Didn't the fire crew have loudspeakers?"

Renata sighed. She had already said far more than she had wanted to. Somehow, revisiting this piece of her childhood, where she could still picture her mother in her mustard yellow cardigan hanging over the wooden railing peering down into the water screaming encouragement — *Vamos, meu amor!* — gave her the feeling that she was unburdening herself to her parents and not to Mick. In the days following that terrible afternoon, she had had no one to speak to. Although they never explicitly blamed her, her husband's parents didn't want to speak to her and were in no position to console her, lost in their own grief. And she could hardly unload to Guil. He was a child, and whether she liked it or not, he was *his* child. *Be careful*, she told herself. *Don't say too much.*

"Dean had a tendency to have long afternoon naps," was all she said, neglecting to mention the fact he was most definitely drunk. "He was an extremely deep sleeper. And apparently the smoke would have killed him before the flames. He may well have passed out before I even ran into the house. I was in and out in seconds and it was even dangerous for me to go in, but I had begged the crew to let me get some photographs of my parents and our passports."

They silently let their feet swing in the air between wood and water.

"Anyway. I am so happy to be back here." Her clipped tone indicated that she was leaving the topic of the fire behind them. "Surrounded on all sides by water. The whole time I was living out there, I would dream of just walking out into the surf and floating over the top of waves. I love that feeling when the wave just lifts you effortlessly up and sets you down again on the sand, on your tippy-toes. It's heaven. The only water out there was a stinky chlorine pool. I hated it. And now I see the ocean from my apartment. *Your* apartment." She fixed Mick with a stern stare. "Which is why you need to promise me to protect it — from squatters *and* storms. I can't become a climate refugee for the second time."

Mick baulked at her choice of words. That's what Sam had called herself — a climate refugee — the night before she left. His disgust in his wife surged with a renewed force. She had not suffered like Renata; she had merely panicked at the potential loss of value in their home and was feeling left out with all her friends decamping to the Central Tablelands. It was hardly on the same level as needing to escape a deadly fire and losing a husband in the process.

He was unsure whether to tell Renata that Sam had gone away, perhaps for good. He could tell she was skittish and would potentially view that revelation as a come-on. He would need to tread carefully.

He waded in gently. "Isn't the bay calm? It hasn't been this still in ages. And it's been a long time since the tide was so low."

The stared together across the bay. Normally, at this time of year, the wattle trees would be drooping with their heavy flaxen floral load, but the recent storms and constant rain had pounded the blossoms off their branches. The ground on the opposite bank was littered with wet petals the colour of fading bruises. The decaying blossoms sent a pungent stink into the air, sticky and rotting.

Mick continued with care. "I could probably walk all the way to my house on the sand right now, the tide is so low."

As expected, she looked at him now with pointed attention, waiting for his next words.

"My house is just down there." He indicated with a swing of his head over his left shoulder.

He watched one of her beautiful eyebrows hike upwards. He'd pushed it too far, had been too obvious.

"I used to date someone who lived in that house there." Her finger was directed at a salmon-coloured house right where the bay curved sharply to the left. "You probably knew him. Josh Levin. He went to a private school in the city, not to our school. I did swimming training with his sister."

"Yeah, we knew the Levins growing up but I didn't know him very well. Like you said, he went to another school and was a bit older."

Renata sighed. "He was my first boyfriend and of course he turned my head a bit with his fancy house. Obviously, he was given a car as soon as he got his licence so he would pick me up and take me for drives through the national park. My mum was probably more impressed than me with his car, the house, the school uniform. Dad saw through him though. And you know what? He was right. My god, he was such a creep. I learned it much too late though."

Renata was surprising Mick for the second time with her candid revelations.

"At first, it was nice. He was my first kiss, my first … everything, actually. But then he started doing really strange things, and I think it was because I was 'just' a Portuguese girl from the local public school. Like he was taunting me or something. Or maybe he was just really socially inept. No idea."

"Like what … what would he do?"

"Once we had spent the afternoon together in his room." Her downcast eyes and slight blush told Mick exactly what they had been doing that afternoon. "His parents came home unexpectedly. He was seventeen, I had just turned sixteen, so it's not like it was totally unexpected that he had a girlfriend over. He got really flustered and asked me to climb out of the window. His room was on the second floor, with a lattice trellis with vines growing all over it under the window. He asked me to climb down and hide next to his car so that he could go downstairs, say hi to his parents, and pretend he was just on his way out to see a friend. I remember crouching by the car and looking through the window at him chatting with his parents and acting like the perfect golden child. I thought to myself, *Wow, they don't know what a jerk he is.* He eventually came out and I had to sneak into the car, duck down low, and then he reversed out of the driveway to drop me home."

Mick shook his head. "Wow."

"Oh but that's nothing compared to what he did later. His parents were away for a weekend and he told me he would like to cook his signature spaghetti bolognaise for me. I was so impressed that he wanted to cook for me; in my family, women do the cooking. It was actually really good and now that I think of it, his mother probably cooked it and left it for him. But I was young and wanted to believe in my first love cooking for me with his own hands. After we ate he cleared the plates and told me he had a surprise for me upstairs."

Mick could not believe the turn this was taking.

"So we went upstairs, and he had put candles all around the bath, and in the middle of the bathroom — it was, of course, a huge bathroom — was a chair." She paused for effect. Mick bent towards her wordlessly.

"I don't need to tell you how romantic sixteen-year-old girls are. I didn't know what was happening but I was intrigued. He asked me to sit on the chair and then he disappeared, coming back a few seconds later with something behind his back. He knelt in front of me."

Wait a minute, thought Mick. *Is she playing me? Does she know how attracted I am to her?* He could not understand why her body language was a definite block to even his most innocent, if clumsy, hints, but this story was going in a decidedly X-rated direction.

"I could hardly breathe. He brought his hands from beyond his back, and I could see he was holding a razor. And then he said: 'Renata, you are such a pretty girl. But I really gotta shave off that moustache.'"

Mick was stunned into silence, searching for some giggle or sign from Renata that would indicate this was an elaborate story she had made up for effect.

"So the result of that, obviously, was that we broke up. I had enough respect for myself — barely — to get out of that bathroom and never go back. But I do think it left me with a rather low bar for future relationships. It basically meant that when I met my husband, he didn't need to do much to woo me. He just needed to let me walk in and out the front door like a normal person. And obviously, not wanting to do anything about my body hair was a huge plus, too."

She paused and looked at Mick pointedly.

"I also made a vow after that day to *never* date anyone who lived on this side of the peninsula."

CHAPTER 8. TINNIE ARMY

Renata dropped Mick back off at the real estate agent, handing him over to an exuberant Rhys and his mound of paperwork. She wound her way through the darkening mall and eastwards towards the Esplanade. The peak of summer had passed, the approaching evening rushing in with varying shades of mauve and chalky pink. As she approached Vaga, she inspected a cluster of surfers sitting cross-legged on the rocks, still barelegged but wrapped in towels and hoodies in the rapidly cooling air. The smell of pot wafted over to her. Guil was not there.

As she pushed open the heavy security door to the Palisade she was surprised to hear his voice coming from the end of the hall, from a large storage room that she had no reason to ever visit. The door to that room was propped open with a small cylinder of gas, allowing the sounds of an animated discussion to spill into the hall. She peeked in to see Guil standing over a group of around ten people, squatting or sitting on the bare floor. Guil seemed to be counting items off a list, using his fingers, while one of the group, a slim woman with her back to the door, scribbled into a notepad.

"Guil?"

"Mum, hey."

"Everything good?"

"Yes, we are just … making some plans."

"Plans for …?"

Guil paused, searching in the corner of the room for words. One of the group, a man just a little younger than Renata, filled the silence.

"We are hoping for the best, but planning for the worst." The group nodded their agreement with this sentiment.

Guil could see that his mother was frustrated with these evasive answers. "OK, Mum, I have been meaning to tell you. We have formed a kind of group, a planning group or team, to get our heads wrapped around how to deal with a huge storm here on the peninsula. A storm like the ones that have been hitting up north. We feel like there are lots of things we can already plan for and get sorted that might be helpful if the worst were ever to happen."

"I think we are called a citizen army — just without training. Or weapons, come to think of it!" The thin woman taking notes laughed as she swivelled around, and Renata was surprised to see it was the elderly lady who lived in her favourite house, the one that Guil had told her was next door to the house of squatters. She had only ever seen her draped in her bathrobe on the wrap-around veranda of her Federation cottage, sipping tea and gazing at the horizon. And yet here she was, in jeans and Ugg boots, looking lively and purposeful as she scribed the meeting.

Guil swept his hand around the circle gathered on the floor. "That's Joe and Ellen from the Glades. And Matt from Sunrise. You remember I was telling you that those apartment blocks are closest to the shore and already have a lot of weather and corrosion damage. And these guys you might recognise from my surfing crew. They squat in the house next to Helen." On hearing her name, Helen, the notetaker, waved cheerily.

"Love, why don't you join us. The more the merrier."

Renata wanted nothing more than to escape upstairs, but seeing her son like this, assertive and self-assured, piqued her interest. She dropped her large handbag onto the floor and slid down next to it. She nodded at Guil to continue.

"OK, where were we?"

"Fuel collection."

"Ah yes. So, we need to have a good supply of petrol we can use for boats and Jet Skis and store it somewhere safe but easily accessible."

"Why not here, in the Palisade? You're set a bit back here from the coast. It's probably the best bet."

"Yeah," agreed Guil. "We could use one of the empty car spaces." He looked pointedly at his mother. "I am sure I will find someone who can donate their space. Leave that with me."

"Maybe best to store that all above ground level though? Anyway, we'll leave that to you, Guil. And should we already start canvassing for boats and Jet Skis we could use?"

Helen's pen scribbled with force on her pad and she led the group through the action items from their last meeting and recorded new ones. Renata realised Guil had been hosting these meetings for at least a few weeks. She sat silently with feelings in equal parts admiration, surprise and increasing alarm as they ran through their topics. They moved from the supply of diesel fuel for boat motors, to the creation of a fleet of stand-by boats and Jet Skis, to the supply of fresh food and water.

"If water levels were to rise even a little more than they did last time, we could be looking at being cut off from the mainland. If that bridge goes under, there is no way we can get through the national park easily. So we have to think about bringing stuff over in boats, or at least having a good store of supplies here locally."

Renata realised this was true. Even though Bombora was a peninsula, not an island, the only access from the mainland was a four-lane bridge at Lilyvale, the same one her father and uncle had worked on years ago. This bridge replaced the much more narrow and picturesque iron bridge that had been sufficient up until the 1970s but which eventually could not cope with the influx of new residents moving to Bombora and who still commuted daily into the city and back. The only other access from Bombora to the mainland was a ninety-minute hike north of the Cove through clumps of mangroves and their hazardous, exposed roots, a hard enough feat even in dry weather let alone during or in the aftermath of a huge storm.

The last topic on the list, Helen announced, concerned evacuation plans for the Glades and Sunrise apartment blocks.

"Joe, Matt, you were going to give us an update."

Joe cleared his throat. "So we had a chat about this earlier this week. We've checked out the elevator shafts as well as we can and we can see that the control panels are in the basement of each building, which is normal for when these elevators were installed, but we understand that modern building codes require that there should be flood-resistant casings around panels and control rooms. There should also be a pump system that kicks in in the event of water flowing in, plus controls that prevent the elevators from descending into floodwater."

Helen paused her scribbling. "Wouldn't people just use the stairs?"

"You can never assume what people might do in a panic situation. And what would happen if the exit to the stairwell was also blocked or obstructed? Plus we have quite a few pensioners living in our buildings, I have no idea how mobile they all are. Regardless, from what we can see, all the electrical boards are below street level, including the fuse boxes for all the apartments, and they aren't up to code. I don't need to remind anyone that water flows downwards."

"We clearly need to engage the owner of the buildings."

Joe scoffed. "If you knew how many times I have been to see that twit at the real estate agency to ask him to put me in touch with the responsible people. They are just avoiding responsibility."

"They clearly don't want to invest too heavily in these buildings. They just want to keep collecting rent as long as they can and minimise their losses."

Renata took in a breath, ready to protest. She, after all, had seen Miele just this very afternoon next to his staggering pile of documents in the real estate office; "maintenance protocols" he had called them. All heads swivelled to her.

"Mum?"

"No, it's OK. I'm just listening."

"Helen, you can just carry over that action for me and Matt. We need a bit more time to do some more digging. But let's assume for evacuation plans that the lifts will definitely be out of order, and we might have a black out as well."

. . . .

The minute they were alone upstairs, Renata erupted.

"What on earth do you think you are doing? Storing petrol, organising boats? Why am I only hearing about this now?"

"Because I knew you would react like this. You are so full of trust that 'someone' has all the plans in order, but I can tell you, Mum — no one does. If disaster hits the peninsula — and why wouldn't it, it's hit everywhere else? — then we are on our own."

"You assured me we were safe here!"

"No, I said there were other buildings less safe than ours. I do believe we are safe here in the Palisade, but that doesn't mean I want to bury my head in the sand and ignore what's going on around me. A lot of my friends are living in houses closer to the shore. And there are hundreds of people living in low lying areas in all the inlets around here who are quite secluded. If anything happens, help might only be able to reach them by boat and that's where I can really help. In fact, all the surfers have signed up to help if needed."

"Listen to you. This is not your job! You haven't even finished school!"

"I can't believe you are acting like this. Where did you meet Dad again? Oh yeah, at the Emergency Services."

"And do I need to remind you why Dad got so sick? Why he got so depressed he could only drink all day, and why we had to move out west so his family could help us survive? Working as a *professional* in an emergency crew. If that can happen to him, what do you think might happen to you? You don't have the training for any of this!"

"Better untrained volunteers than no one. Because those are the only options."

Renata felt her panic rise. She had never encountered Guil like this. He was completely unmoved by her. Since Dean had died, he had bent over backwards to indulge her wherever possible. The minute she had said she wanted to move back to Bombora, he was fully onboard to help make it happen. If she wanted company, he would cancel his surfing plans and stay with her. He was available for running chores, he was thoughtful and considerate. But now he stood steely eyed at the kitchen island and had a rebuttal to every argument she brought forward.

"Your father ended up dying because of his job as a rescue worker."

Guil clenched his fists.

"My father died because you didn't see him asleep out the back. Which I have always been curious about, actually."

Renata froze. She felt her cheeks go hot, felt a tightening in her throat as if invisible hands were squeezing.

Guil continued. "You always said we would talk about that afternoon, but we never have. So why not right now?"

She struggled to get her words out through her constricted throat. "I'm not sure there is much more to tell you. You know what happened. It was all such a rush."

"Mum, we both know that there was a simple way to know if Dad was at home or not. His thongs at the front door. If they were gone, it meant he had walked over to Nana and Pop. If they were there, it meant he was in the house. They have never *not* meant that he was there. It was our code. You taught me that."

It was true. From the time they had moved out west and Dean's behaviour had become more erratic, when he really started descending into his paranoias and anxieties and when the drinking accelerated, Renata had started to teach her son how to develop and use the kind of radar she assumed would always keep them safe. Thongs gone: you can breathe a sigh of relief. Thongs by the doormat: he's here, be quiet, don't bang doors or yell, tread carefully.

He continued. "We had the car so we knew he was not out. That leaves two options; he was at home or he had gone over to Nan and Pop's."

"What exactly are you implying? That I deliberately left him? That I *knew* he was there?"

The most uncomfortable twenty seconds of Renata's life followed. Guil blinked at her, tiny muscles in his jaw twitching. The younger Guil, the needier Guil, would have rushed forward and hugged her, assuring her that he could never have entertained such a thought, begging forgiveness for even having given her that impression. This Guil, this purposeful and sure Guil, who just minutes ago had been directing the actions of ten untrained and eager volunteers, most of them Renata's own age, stood firm and held her gaze steadily.

Those long seconds throbbed in the darkening room. Each one heralded an unwelcome realisation, as sure and steady as a nail being hammered into fresh and yielding timber. The fact that Guil could have perceived those events as anything other than what she had reported to him terrified her. The malleable child was long gone; a strong, young man stood in front of her, silhouetted against the glass doors framing the indigo evening sky.

She cleared her throat. "I had to beg to run back into the house. The crew insisted you stay in the car and they told me I had no more than a few minutes. They told me if I wasn't back by then, they would take you with them. We were the last house to be evacuated because we'd been at the pool, remember?"

He nodded. It was he who had insisted they go swimming that day even though the smoke had turned the sky into a crackling, toxic bruise. The morning's radio report had predicted the path of the fire, which had been burning for days, would continue west and away from their suburb. It was only while they were at the pool that the wind had changed and forced the fire back into the opposite direction and into a fresh supply of dry bush, a runway directly towards the cul-de-sac where they lived. The speed at which the fire started to move surprised everyone. Renata remembered watching Guil splashing around and suddenly seeing ash flakes the size of ten cent coins alighting on the hairs of her forearms.

"One of the crew wrapped a damp cloth around my face before I ran in. The smoke had gotten so thick by that point so it was a condition for me to be able to go back in. It covered my whole face except for my eyes, and that together with the smoke meant I could barely see. I found our passports and my parents' albums by muscle memory alone. My heart was pounding and I just wanted to get back to you safely."

"So you didn't see his thongs?"

"I did not see his thongs."

What she didn't say was this, the smoke had been so thick she had not even *seen* the framed photos hanging on the walls, but they were undoubtedly there. She also hadn't *seen* the door handle on the way into their home, her hand had simply reached into the smokey haze until her fingers had found it (the door was always unlocked, whether anyone was home or not, as was usual during the day in their cul-de-sac). Just as well, her shaking hands would not have been able to navigate a key and lock.

Asking her whether she had *seen* or *not seen* anything was not the right question. She wasn't lying to Guil when she said she hadn't seen his father's thongs by the front door. She had known full well they might have been there. The reality was, she could have squatted down and felt around for them. He often kicked them off so hard that they flew back against the wall and settled partly obscured by a large potted palm by the door.

And she hadn't; she had chosen not to. But this was not the question that Guil had asked her. No one had asked her that directly, not even Dean's parents. People only heard *time pressure, smoke, hurry, damp cloth, child alone in car, crew yelling, panic, escape, survival.* No one had or ever would accuse Renata of having been negligent. And it appeared now that Guil, who was standing right at the precipice of a more nuanced reality than had ever been openly discussed, either didn't think of pursuing it or decided not to.

He opened his arms and she welcomed his embrace, but even with her face pressed into the soft plushness of his hoodie, she was aware of the fault line they had crossed. She wondered if he felt it too.

. . . .

Later in bed, thoughts closed in on Renata in nebulous clouds. She had to admit a feeling of relief; finally Guil had pressed, had asked her bluntly about what exactly had happened in the few minutes she had been away from him on the day of the fire. She felt an urgent wave of love and concern for that little boy who had no doubt pressed his face against the window of the car and had waited anxiously for her to reemerge through the smoke. She let a new thought descend and settle upon her, like the coin-sized ash flakes from that afternoon; he would have been waiting for two figures to come stumbling out of the house towards the car. He would have been hoping desperately for it.

As adult as he had just been standing over her in their kitchen, or downstairs commandeering a newly formed "tinnie army", on the day of the fire he had still been a child. He had clung to the fantasy of a daddy who could get better, who could be saved, who could make Mummy laugh again, who could have been pulled by one hand out of the fire into the car and into safety. She realised now the grief that he must have been feeling, not just for a father who had perished in the flames, but for the family of three that could never be put back together again. She had thought she was sparing him pain by withholding the details of his father's mental health decline; she had simply taught him the new codes to live by, signs to be on the lookout for in order to stay out of the path of danger. She had forgotten that a child will always yearn for a parent, no matter how unpredictable or erratic their behaviour. Every time they had escaped for an evening walk, Renata had patted herself on the back for protecting her child from an intoxicated father and a potentially explosive or violent situation. She was a Good Mother. Now she realised Guil quite possibly resented the separation she was causing and the ever escalating two-against-one constellation of their family which became absolutely final on the afternoon of the fire. Two survived, one had not.

She sat up in bed with a thumping heart, the sound of waves swelling and sucking at the rock shelf far below. She was not the victim and saviour that everyone assumed her to be. She had been a frightened woman who had justifiable (so she thought) reasons to believe her husband's simmering aggression would one day be unleashed upon his son, especially now that he was on that critical cusp of manhood.

Guil had stepped away from any final accusations. He had accepted it when Renata had said she had not *seen* any thongs. This, she realised, was not a successful deception on her part. It was a sign of compassion on his.

· · · ·

On the other side of the wall, Guil was curled into his usual tight knot on his bed, eyes wide and staring. Ever since his father had died he had struggled to fall asleep. The only technique that seemed to help was to buttress himself as much as possible against the still, impassive air of his bedroom. He took to sleeping with a hoodie drawn tight around his face which, together with the covers pulled up under his chin, left only a narrow sliver of face exposed. Balled up under his layers of cotton and fleece, even on warm nights, his hands were constantly active as he methodically and absently picked at the skin around his fingernails. He barely winced as the skin tore.

He knew that sleep would be especially elusive on this night. He might have successfully swallowed down the angry words he had wanted to unload on his mother, but now they lay like stones under his ribcage, pulsing with heat that radiated all the way up to his cheeks through the constricted tunnel of his throat. He could hear waves exploding against the rock shelf far below and wished it was already sunrise so he could slide on his wetsuit and slink away into the grey morning. The salt and waves were the only things that could loosen his tight muscles and melt his anxiety.

His mother never noticed his raw fingers, or the heavy bags under his eyes. She never seemed to look properly at him at all. He knew she often sat at the front bar of Vaga and watched him surf, but she did not seem to want to look at him up close — only from a safe, blurry distance. He easily embodied the image of a perfect teenage boy when he was reduced to a mere black outline dipping and breaching in the waves. She wafted about as if in a daze in Bombora, floating in her summer dresses between her job (she had been given her old role back at the Emergency Services), the supermarket, the beach, and their apartment, happily chirping about the beautiful beach, the parks, the great coffee.

Their recent life out west, and the events immediately preceding their return to Bombora, were an unspoken taboo.

In fact, the ease with which she seemed to slip back into her old life made Guil furious, as if their few years away were just an unfortunate blip in the chosen trajectory of her life. All calm was now apparently restored, leaving Guil alone to try to reconcile the huge chasm between his mother's version of events and his own uncertain, but persistent, perceptions.

It was not only the day of the fire that bothered him. He also now questioned many moments and rituals they had had out west. He remembered the way she would come and snatch him away from his homework the minute his father came home so that they could go for a walk, not even giving him a chance to assess for himself if his father was in a reasonable mood or not. The many nights that he and his mother had eaten dinner early — too early, in Guil's opinion — leaving a plate for his father to eat alone. Although Renata obscurely hinted that there was some potential danger that made all of this necessary, Guil now — with the benefit of a bit of distance — realised that he personally had never felt unsafe around his father. Uncomfortable, yes; but that had more to do with the strange dynamic between his parents and very little to do with his own relationship with him. His father drank, that was a fact (and it had drastically accelerated after the incident that had forced them to move out west) but so too did the Vaga crowd, spilling out onto the concrete Esplanade every single afternoon and evening when Guil was coming in from his after-school surf. What was the difference, exactly? That the crowd here in Bombora drank wine and cocktails and dressed up to get drunk, and his father had over-indulged on supermarket-branded beer in the comfort of his own home?

As a young boy, he had felt protected by his mother. Now, alone in his bedroom, he just felt robbed of his father.

Renata was impossible to speak to. She fell back on the grief of losing her parents in such quick succession, and now on the trauma of the fire (although in his worst moments Guil suspected she was secretly grateful to have had an opportunity to come back to Bombora) and thereby averted any tough discussions. If Guil started making signals that he might like to talk, her eyelashes would dampen and she would press a hand to her forehead, her sign to stop probing. But on this matter, his tinnie army, Guil would not be deterred. He pulled a long flake of skin from around his thumb and felt a stinging pain as raw skin was exposed to the dark, still air. He was positive his father would have approved.

CHAPTER 9. THE KIDS

Mick waited until Sam had been gone a few weeks before reaching out to his children. She had been away for a similar time period many times before and also often at short notice, usually with a handful of girlfriends for a workshop or retreat of some kind. When he could be bothered to ask for details, he was often completely confused by the premise of some of these trips. He recalled a tantric dance fortnight in Ubud, after which she had come home with two kilo bags of what must have been the world's most expensive cacao. Spittle had flown from his mouth as he laughed theatrically. "That's not the usual two kilo shipment flowing from Bali to Australia!"

"We did cacao ceremonies and *danced*!" she had said defensively. "I brought back some cacao so I can do some ceremonies here." The two bags were still unopened at the back of one of the overhead kitchen cupboards together with a set of ceremonial pewter cups and spoons still wrapped in tissue paper.

There had been a ridiculously expensive week at a resort in Broome with daily silent walking meditations and vocal workshops to soothe the vagus nerve.

"What was the point of *that*?" Mick had asked, irritated after having seen the charges she had put on their credit card.

"To heal trauma," Sam had answered simply.

"What exact trauma are you trying to rid yourself of, Sam? What's wrong with your life?" He had held his hands wide to indicate the gleaming kitchen around them, as if perfectly coordinated kitchen appliances were in and of themselves a worthy display of self-actualisation.

In retrospect, Mick could understand that she had eventually stopped telling him about her various trips. It had become an accepted part of their marriage, especially once the children had moved out, that with little explanation she might just disappear for a couple of weeks. It was no exception this time; he expected she would be back at some point, with a suitcase full of charms and totems and ready to either resume their dysfunctional relationship or sit down and finally discuss whether they should separate. The extreme toxicity of their last argument was still fresh in Mick's mind. He personally hoped that she would *not* come back with promises of soothed vagus nerves, a daily yoga practice, or a vision board full of glossy magazine clippings and motivational phrases. Over the last few weeks he had been free to concentrate on his work with no dread of what mood he would find his wife in when night fell. He felt relieved.

He had also been freed up to concentrate on his budding friendship with Renata. Since their afternoon at the baths, Renata and Mick had been meeting periodically for a coffee at Vaga. A polar opposite to Sam, Renata was even-keeled and serious, occasionally even dour, but Mick was rediscovering the kick of long, meandering conversations that did not inevitably escalate into a screaming match. Renata was clear that she was not in the market for a relationship, and he believed her, yet she was stirring up in him a yearning for a fresh, clean-slate relationship, one that was an intoxicating dance, a progressive dropping of the veils.

He had never had this with Sam. They had been school mates, fused together from their early teens. They had awkwardly stumbled through puberty together, sharing friends, mix cassettes, sports fields, and families. He had never *not* known Sam. There had never been a thrill of discovery or a delight in her "newness". This is what he now realised he desperately wanted, and Renata was ticking all of those boxes. She was not simply a new enigma to unpack, but she spoke of foreign foods, places, languages and ideas. For once, Mick did not feel he needed to be the expert on every topic and he was not being constantly asked to fix or provide something; he could just lean back and enjoy the new and novel rolling over him, like fresh spring water.

Mick dialled Adele's number first.

"Hey, kiddo. Happy I caught you."

"You'll have to make it quick. I'm walking to my next lecture." Mick could hear the animated chatter and laughter of the students around Adele. He pictured her cutting her way through the elegant quadrangle of Sydney University, stepping over clusters of students lounging on the grass while they ate or hurriedly prepared for their next lecture. He had never been to university and had been so impressed when they had visited Adele during her orientation week, admiring the covered walkways around the old sandstone buildings and the perfectly trimmed lawns. He had felt a slight regret that he had charged straight from school into his father's business and had never had this opportunity to waft around from lecture hall to lawn, from lawn to library. Adele had laughed when he had once expressed this to her, assuring him that she personally had little time to lie around on the grass and that he was being overly romantic.

"I just wanted to know if you've heard from your mother. I think she went away on one of her soul journeys but I haven't heard from her in a while."

"Well, if you are always that condescending about it, I am not surprised she hasn't told you where she is."

"Adele, please just tell me if she has called you." Mick knew that Sam kept regular contact with both children; she was, when all was said and done, an excellent mother.

"Yes, she did call me from John and Nat's but I think she may have moved on from there now. She made plans to come and see me this weekend and she hasn't cancelled, so I assume she'll be back before the end of the week."

"And she is all right?"

"All right? I don't know about that. She didn't go into details, but I assume you two have been fighting again." She paused. "It seems a strange question for you to be asking me, if Mum is *all right*. What do you think? You live with her. What do *your* perceptions tell you?"

Mick could hear that Adele must have found an empty stairwell or nook in which to continue their conversation. The ambient sounds of students calling to each other dropped away and he could hear a new echo over the line. He pictured his slim daughter standing in shadows with books clutched to her chest, the tone in her voice telling him her face was pinched and concentrated in an expression Mick knew well.

"She's upset about all her friends leaving Bombora and she wants us to sell up and leave too. We had a bit of a heated discussion about that."

"Mmmm."

"What do you think? Do you think it's come to that?"

"I think it's interesting that the two of you think that climate change is the crisis going on in your life. There are other things much closer to home that I am surprised you never address."

"Meaning?"

"Come on, Dad. Mum's drinking. *Jesus.*"

Mick was uncharacteristically lost for words. Adele continued. "I know you look down your nose every time Mum goes to one of her workshops. Personally, I am always relieved because it means she has to take a break from the drinking and it also indicates that she is searching for something. She is clearly not happy but she is not distracting herself from it, she's looking for answers. You really should be more supportive."

"I am supportive. Who do you think pays for it all?"

"That's not the kind of support I am talking about, and you know it. Don't you think it's ironic that she uses *your* money to pay other people to listen to her, when you could do it for free?"

A peal of bells sounded out on Adele's side of the line.

"Shit," she muttered. "I really have to go. I'll tell you if I hear from Mum again. You should check with Ethan too. If you call him now you'll catch him before he starts work."

Mick held the phone in his hand for several minutes. Adele had not been at home to witness Sam's recent escalation in drinking, but he knew she was referring to a habit that stretched back through the years. She had not gone so far as to label him an enabler but her implication was clear. He had a flashback to Adele as a skinny child in her pyjamas at the dinner table, glaring at Mick while he topped up Sam's wine glass and then stomping off to bed furiously when her mother fell asleep in front of the television, her face a worried little knot.

He dialled Ethan's number, already braced to receive more of the same lecture from his son.

"She's in Tasmania," Ethan stated simply once Mick had moved past the pleasantries and asked if he had heard from his mother.

"Tasmania? Doing what?"

"She has a cousin down there who has a bee farm. Jay? She says we have only met him once or twice when we were really little. Why don't you know this?"

"She was a bit upset when she left. We didn't get a chance to discuss it."

"Yeah, she wants you to sell up, right? Not a bad idea if you ask me."

"Why do you say that?"

"You need to protect your investments. Seems like the ship is going down and it's better to get out sooner rather than later."

"You sound very pragmatic, son. You would honestly be fine with me selling the home you and Adele grew up in?"

"Don't be offended but I don't feel overly attached to that house, Dad."

Mick snorted. In calling his children to make sure Sam was okay, he seemed to be uncovering all sorts of interesting clues as to their opinion about him. "What exactly is wrong with the house, Ethan?"

"It's a lovely house. A very adult house. Great for entertaining." Mick could faintly hear Ethan lighting up a cigarette and exhaling. "Look. I just think you need to take the long-term view here. Ultimately this is not just about you and Mum. Adele and I should also have a say in this. I mean, it's our inheritance you are playing with here."

"Wow."

"Come on, don't be offended that I said that. I am just saying the consequences of you acting or not acting go further than just you and Mum. I don't think living right on the coast is sustainable, and that being the case, why protract things? Look at how many of your friends have already gone. All smart people."

"None of you seem to have any trust in me to be able to protect our home, and maybe Bombora with it."

Ethan's famous temper kicked into gear. "For fuck's sake Dad, you are good at many things but you are not invincible. I know you feel like you built Bombora single-handedly but you did so under very different circumstances. It was a different era. People were basically flat-earthers, developing every scrap of land with no regard to the environment. But we know better now. Stop ignoring the obvious."

For the second time in ten minutes, Mick was being told he was "ignoring the obvious", albeit for two very different reasons. Knowing he was being childish, he made an excuse for ending the conversation and the two men tersely signed off. He leaned back in his office chair, the leather creaking under his weight, and sighed. He wished he had enjoyed his children more when they had had nothing but adoration for him, pouncing on him when he came home from work damp from their baths. He would collapse in one of the living room chairs, Adele's tiny fingers trying to unknot his tie and Ethan carefully sliding off his leather shoes and lining them up in the hall. It wasn't hard to feel like a king when your children thought it was fun to brush talc off your toes and usher you barefoot to the dinner table.

Everyone in Bombora relied on Mick, whether it was fund-raising, setting up business deals, or pulling wayward sharks out of rock pools. His family, however, only seemed to find him lacking.

CHAPTER 10. FAREWELL PARTY

It was a night Mick had not been looking forward to. Lou had decided to throw one last bash at Vaga before closing the doors for good. Negotiations with the insurance company had gone nowhere; the premium, if he were to pay it, would represent the largest fixed cost for keeping the restaurant open and would wipe out a large portion of his profit. He was still out of pocket for the damage the last king tide had caused, even though it was not exorbitant; only one pane of glass had cracked and needed replacing. However, on top of the prohibitive insurance Lou had noticed that custom was also falling. More and more of his loyal customer base had moved away. The large group bookings for long lunches had disappeared and he would never make as much revenue selling coffees to the ever-expanding mob of cash-strapped surfers who hung out on the rock platform in front of Vaga.

Mick had shared many a coffee in previous days with Lou, Mick listening supportively as his friend bemoaned the reversal of his fortunes. "The final nail in the coffin was your wife leaving," joked Lou wryly. "The grog bills alone from her lunches were the lion's share of my takings some weeks." Lou was one of the few people with whom Mick spoke openly about his wife's decampment. Even though by now most people in Bombora knew, not many would have been brave enough to broach the subject directly to Mick's face.

"Who are you going to invite?" Mick had asked. "Are there enough people left to invite at all?"

"Well I might have to loosen the criteria a little, mate. It's come to this; I'll probably just hang an open invitation on the front door. One last party to get rid of all the stock I have left." He paused and tapped a spoon lightly against his espresso cup. "It's really changed around here, hasn't it?"

Mick nodded. Since Renata had spoken to him about her anxiety of squatters, his eyes were suddenly open to the significant shift that Bombora had undergone right in front of him. The neat packs of power-walking pensioners tugging designer dogs on leashes through the mall had given way to a much more diverse population. People had moved here from the flood-ravaged towns up north, snapping up properties from landlords at much lower rents than they had ever thought possible. There were also families who had moved in from the west who, like Renata, had had enough of the droughts and endless water restrictions. They knew that Bombora and other seaside towns like it held their own climate dangers. But at least, while waiting for disaster to strike, they could enjoy the ocean and the infrastructure of what had once been a prohibitively expensive, exclusive beachside suburb. There was even some snobby pride in being able to finally say, "I live in Bombora."

There were digital nomads who treated Bombora as an interesting place to hang out temporarily, never planning to put down permanent roots and willing to play a careful game of timing in deciding exactly how long to stay. At the first hint of a big storm moving down from the north, they could pack up and head slightly inland, only to return once the storm had passed.

So many long-term rentals had been flipped into Airbnb listings that this seat-of-the-pants planning was entirely possible. There were even, he had learned, climate thrill-seekers who came here specifically because the storms were getting more and more Instagrammable. There were young women in bikinis who stood in front of Vaga while huge waves crashed against the rock wall behind them, framing them in photogenic foamy spray, and drones that buzzed above the surfers during high swells to capture footage that could be sold to global streaming platforms.

On the night of Lou's party, Mick planned to stop by for one drink to show support and then head off. Lou had indeed hung a general invitation on the front door of the restaurant and so the place was packed with a noisy melange of locals and people Mick had never seen before. Some had dressed up, some were in sports clothes, most wore shoes, some didn't. And there at the extravagantly tiled bar, with her freshly washed hair in fluffy curls around her shoulders, stood Renata with her son. A quick scan of the room revealed there was no one else he knew there yet to speak to. He cut a path through the crowd towards her, breathing in the smell of her green apple shampoo as he approached. Guil eyed him warily as Renata flicked her hair over her shoulder and shuffled a little to the left to make room for him.

"I must admit, I did not expect to find you here," he said awkwardly while nodding solemnly at an unsmiling Guil.

"You're right, this is not my usual scene. But I had to come. My father and uncle helped build this place. Guil and I were just admiring the incredible workmanship of this bar. Look at the tiles! So tiny." Her long fingers circled over the iridescent surface, affection and pride glowing in her eyes.

"Mate, you made it." Lou erupted from the crowd beside them, large damp sweat patches under each arm. "Think I'll move all my stock tonight after all! Look at this turn-out. Someone will be around soon with the cocktails."

He clicked his fingers across the room at a tiny waitress struggling to make her way through the crowd with a tray of flute glasses filled with a lurid coloured liquid. Draping his arm over Mick's shoulders and giving him a little shake of affection, he lowered his voice to confide, "The staff came up with a signature cocktail using the bottles we had left over. Personally, I would ask for beer or wine. Unless you have nothing important to do tomorrow and fancy a day in bed."

"Have you met Renata? She was just telling me that her father and uncle helped fit out this space."

"I do indeed remember them!" boomed Lou. "They are the reason we named the place Vaga. Something to do with 'heat-wave' in Portuguese, right? Pleasure to officially meet you. I've seen you in here a few times having coffee over there." Lou nodded towards the bar stools facing out towards the sea.

"You do remember though, that Vaga was not their first suggestion for a name? Actually, my father had recommended 'Piscina', which means 'pool'."

"That would have been fitting. Can't remember that name ever being on the table, to be honest."

"After road-testing the name with a couple of locals, he realised the Aussie pronunciation made it sound a little off-colour."

Lou's thick lips silently mouthed the words to himself. "Ah shit, yeah. I see."

"Piss in 'er", deadpanned Renata.

"Mum!" exclaimed Guil.

Mick clapped a hand over his mouth, his eyes crinkling in laughter.

"So you can see why Vaga was chosen in the end. Not so easy to butcher. Although, funnily enough, you would not believe the other meaning to the word. It doesn't just originate from the word 'heatwave'." She paused for effect. Guil looked at her warily, not recognising this version of his mother who could be crude and was naturally holding Mick and Lou in her thrall. They both leaned down towards her expectantly.

"It also means 'vacancy'."

"Oh." Lou straightened. "Well, well. Yes, very prophetic."

"I'm sorry, I didn't mean to be rude. It must be devastating to have to pack up after so long."

"It's been a great ride. I've seen weddings, christenings, birthdays, anniversaries. Sports clubs awards nights, book launches. Post-Sunday football parties." Lou and Mick exchanged a look. "Remember when Stu Riley got sprung in the toilet with ..."

Mick pushed a finger against his lips. "Shhh, mate. Ladies present."

"What will happen with the space now, do you reckon?" asked Guil.

"Dunno. Maybe the surf club will use it as storage. I'm quite sure no one will get the insurance needed to run it as a proper cafe or restaurant again. Maybe a pop-up, they're all the rage aren't they? Some sort of street kitchen thing? Don't you kids love all that?" He swivelled towards Guil. "Tacos, burritos. Something you can pack up in five minutes and piss off if the weather looks grim."

"What about this bar?" Renata was still running one hand over the tiles.

"It can't be disassembled easily. It's a slab of cement under all those tiles. I guess it will all just sit here until someone demolishes the whole space. It's not even worth trying to get all the tiles off, they are so small. They'd probably break if you tried to remove them."

"Who owns this place anyway?" asked Guil.

"A guy called Gary, but he's gone, haven't seen him in months. Like most owners and developers. Moved on to greener, dryer pastures. I've been pretty loyal, continuing to pay rent on time every month but I have often wondered what would happen if I had stopped. I have no idea where he is, or whether he's written off all his investments in Bombora."

A woman with a pile of rust-red dyed hair in stiff curls atop her head pushed past them towards the serving area of the bar. Lou greeted her and made room for her to join them. Long, green earrings dropped down the length of her well-tanned face to graze her shoulders and she was draped in a floor length kaftan with a thick smattering of sequins over her generous bust. She was a chameleon who blended perfectly with the glittering bar next to her.

"Hey, Jackie, you also rent from Gary Hesslop, right?"

"Yup, sure do."

"And? Have you heard anything from him?"

"Nothing. I sent a termination of rental agreement to his post office box weeks ago but haven't heard back. I'm moving all my stock out next week."

"You're closing up shop too? But you're relatively protected up there in the mall, I would imagine?"

"It's not because of the weather. Well, not directly. How many people do you think want to come and buy frocks such as this?" With her two hands, she lifted the sides of her kaftan up like wings, the sheer fabric revealing the silhouette of her pillowy figure underneath. "These gowns used to be *de rigueur* for all the ladies around here. The perfect loungewear for sundowners and dinners. But where have all my customers gone? I would love to know." She suddenly fixed Mick with an intense stare, her cobalt eyelids wrinkling thickly. "Maybe you know! Where is Sam?"

All eyes swivelled to Mick, including a few people outside of their group who had been following their discussion.

"Well, she's been in touch with the kids, obviously. They tell me she hasn't settled anywhere, she's just visiting some friends and looking at different areas. Taking a break. She was pretty worked up before she left. Strung out, not eating." *Drinking plenty though.*

"But has she *left* you?" Jackie was as unapologetic in her bluntness as she was in her extravagant dress sense. Renata regarded Mick silently. She remembered Sam, a tall, freckly netballer from their school. Although she had avoided asking Mick about his homelife, she had assumed his wife was still here somewhere. The various onlookers outside of their little circle shuffled closer.

"We have not had a discussion about that. She's made it clear she is not happy living here anymore. What that means for our home and my businesses is an open question. I've just been giving her space to cool off. I know she'll be back eventually. She only left with a couple of bags and her mother is still here in The Pines nursing home." He paused to sip the beer that Lou had pushed into his hand. "She'll have to come back and sort things out eventually." *I can wait.*

Jackie lifted a bangle-laden arm to rest on Mick's shoulder. "Well anyway, I miss her. She was a great customer, she and all her friends. Not sure where my next target market for Balinese kaftans is going to come from. Perhaps it's time to make a switch. Candles, ceramics."

"Even that won't work around here. The people moving in these days don't buy fancy bowls and smelly candles. Look at them." This came from a tall, sinewy woman who had been listening to the conversation from the periphery and had now secured a spot in their ever-expanding semi-circle.

They all twisted to look in the direction she indicated. Renata recognised several of Guil's surfing crew perched on her favourite stools by the window. They were throwing back the free cocktails, with a cluster of empty glasses collecting between them.

"That's going to make for some fluorescent puke a bit later," sighed Lou. Then he perked up. "But hey! It won't be my job to hose it off the pavement anymore."

"They don't eat at the restaurants, or buy homewares, or Tupperware, or go to personal trainers, or support any of the local businesses here," continued the tall newcomer, her voice nasal and brackish. Mick recognised her; she was a massage therapist who did home visits. He'd seen her several times bringing her fold-up bed into the house and heading upstairs to their bedroom, slinking out again ninety minutes later. He had always wondered why Sam had never emerged in a better mood afterwards.

"Oh my God, look at them *now*."

One of the surfers, no doubt wanting to avoid the long queue that was forming inside Vaga for the toilet, had grabbed an ice bucket and taken it outside and placed it in the shadows. He aimed his arc of urine into the bucket where it landed acoustically and with a large amount of splash back, his bare butt cheeks illuminated by the light spilling out of the restaurant. His friends cheered and captured the show on their phones.

"*Animals.*"

Guil bristled visibly. Renata lay a hand gently on his forearm and squeezed but he was not deterred. "You better hope you don't need their help one of these days."

The tall masseuse looked indignant. "What help could I possibly need from *them?*"

"You've just been whining about how all your customers — the 'good' ones, the 'rich' ones — have all moved away. Why do you think that is? Do you think it might have something to do with the increasingly wild weather?"

"Well, yes, of course ..."

"But *you* are still here, taking your chances — like we all are. Hoping that if we stay, the next storm won't be as bad as we fear, or that it will bypass us altogether. It's a massive gamble. You should think of those guys — my friends — as your insurance policy in the event it doesn't play out the way we hope." With that, Guil broke away from the group and pushed through the crowd towards his friends at the window.

"What on earth is he talking about? I have insurance, real insurance ..."

Lou scoffed. "You better check that it is still valid. Why do you think I'm closing up here? The insurance is unpayable. First they screw businesses like mine, but at some point even private homes here will be denied proper cover."

"It's true," sighed Jackie, fondling the skirt of her kaftan reflectively. "I have heard people say that they wish the mother of all storms would come in the next few months, before all the insurance premiums go up or policies are cancelled altogether. At least then they would get compensated properly for any losses."

"Something tells me that even if that did happen, the insurance companies would have a thousand reasons why they won't pay. '*You left the window open and the water got in.*'" Lou's face showed clearly what he thought of insurance companies.

Renata spoke up. "Forget insurance, what Guil is talking about is what actually happens *during* one of these storms. Your insurance is worth nothing if you haven't survived it."

"We have our own council services, what do we need from *that* pack of kids?"

"I wouldn't have so much blind faith in our council if I were you," muttered Mick, setting his empty beer glass down on the bar.

Lou leaned in to whisper in Mick's ear. "Easy tiger, Rodney is over there." Mick twisted his head to see Bombora's mayor perched at a low table looking uncomfortable, staring dubiously at the cocktail glass that had been placed down in front of him. His glum-faced wife sat next to him. Mick was suddenly like a Doberman tugging on a leash, straining to get through the crowd towards Rodney with Lou unsuccessfully holding him back, both hands clasping his bicep.

Mick yanked over a free stool and wedged himself between Rodney and his wife. "How nice that you've shown up to Vaga's living wake, the latest example of your completely incompetent climate change planning for the peninsula."

"Not now, mate, this is a social evening. If you want to talk business you can make an appointment."

"I've been trying to get in to see you for weeks. Funny, I don't remember it being so hard to get time on your calendar when I was dropping off proceeds from the fundraising Sam and I were constantly doing for you." The small circle that Mick had been standing in at the bar — Lou, Kaftan Jackie, the sour-faced masseuse, and Renata — all shuffled along the bar as discreetly as they could to remain within earshot.

Rodney sighed. "A lot of people fundraise for us, Mick. We have kindergarten kids selling cookies door to door. We have old ladies making botanical calendars to sell at Christmas time. That doesn't mean they work for the council or have any right to tell us how to do our jobs." Even the mayor's wife cringed at his unfortunate comparisons between Mick, kindergartners and old ladies. Sensing what was to come, she grabbed her cocktail glass and evacuated the table.

Renata noticed that when Mick got angry, he became menacingly quiet. He leaned towards Rodney. She saw his fingers curl into a tight fist, the knuckles straining and white. The group at the bar struggled to hear.

"Look around this room, mate. This is the new Bombora. Half of our old friends have left. The ones that are still here are figuring out how long they can hang on for. Businesses are closing, people are losing their jobs, and no one believes that when the next storm hits they are going to get any real assistance from you. You've sat on your hands for long enough. You've done nothing to protect Bombora from what's coming."

"What's coming, Mick? We've always had storms. You've all got short memories. I've got black and white photos at home of some of the storms our parents and grandparents experienced. And guess what? We dealt with it, we moved on. Ebb and flow, mate."

"Ah yes, speaking of our forefathers. If you had read the vulnerability report I had commissioned, you would see that some of the lowest lying land we've got here in Bombora is the cemetery. Even that hasn't spurred you to action? Can you imagine what would happen if the coffins ..."

Renata took a sharp intake of breath; both of her parents were laid to rest there. Lou pressed his hands down on Mick's shoulders. "Okay, enough mate. No need to get too graphic."

Mick continued. "My point is, other councils have successfully put a whole range of measures in place. I know we can't sandbag the ocean facing side of the peninsula, but we could be proactively protecting the bay side and all the inlets, and creating more and more housing over there. Housing that's affordable, not just more and more McMansions. Which by the way, are mostly sitting empty right now. Come to my street any night of the week and you'll see how few lights are on."

"We don't have money in the bank for those sorts of measures. What you're talking about involves buybacks, and massive new development."

"It's not the bank that's empty, Rodney, you complete tool. It's your lack of imagination and vision that's the problem." He tapped his finger against his temple. "It's up here that's empty, mate."

"And you're just another naive, rich overlord who thinks that because you have money — and you've made *a lot* of money from this community, Mick — you can boss around the rest of us. You cannot just dictate to me what our council works on. Thanks for throwing a few parties at the yacht club, much appreciated. But that's where your involvement ends. I suggest you focus on your problems a little closer to home." To illustrate his point, Rodney cocked his hand at his forehead, a caricature of a sailor seeking land.

"Sam, Sam? No? Not here. Funny, she used to rule the roost here. I'm sure Lou is really going out of business because she's not on the pinot grigio anymore."

Even Lou could not move fast enough to prevent Mick's fist swinging through the air and landing with a sickening crunch in the centre of Rodney's face.

Mick clasped his fist as it started to throb. "There you go. I've always called you Rodney Fuckface behind your back, and now you have one. My pleasure. That's the last thing you'll ever get for free from me."

CHAPTER 11. AFTER PARTY

Mick perched on a stool in Renata's apartment cradling a hand that was wrapped in a tea towel full of ice cubes.

"That was a nice, clean break, mate," muttered Lou, his huge frame hunched on the stool next to him. Renata winced each time he shifted, the slender wooden legs of the stool squealing under his weight. These stools had only ever held the comparatively slender frames of Renata and Guil and had not been road tested on someone with the mass of Lou. Renata, stool-less, leaned against a kitchen bench.

Mick was unapologetic. "I hope he's sitting up in the emergency department right now. I hope there's at least twenty people waiting in front of him and that he sits there all night. I hope someone next to him has a vile respiratory illness and coughs all over him. Then, I hope there is only an intern available to fix his nose. Badly. So that his crooked nose can forever be a symbol of his total incompetence."

"Bastard traitor," agreed Lou, shifting and releasing a wail from the stool. "Good thing you didn't have the roll of coins in your hand," Lou whispered to Mick. "His nostrils would be on backwards now if that was the case."

"Roll of coins?" asked Renata, perplexed.

"Shhh," hissed Mick to Lou. "Nothing Renata, just ignore this guy." The last thing Mick wanted at this point was for Renata to think he was a common thug.

Lou continued. "And what he said about Sam. He was wrong there. She preferred chardonnay to pinot grigio."

Mick swivelled sharply towards Lou.

"Mate, it was a joke. I'm just trying to lighten the mood." Lou patted Mick's shoulder with his oversized hand.

"Renata, do you have a shot of anything? I feel like we all need a soother."

Renata opened a cupboard, standing on tiptoes to see what was at the back. She was barefoot, her dress riding up to reveal her tanned, sinewy calf muscles that twitched as she tried to stretch herself longer. Mick was aware that Lou was also looking.

"I think I could have something back here."

Mick thought of the massive amounts of alcohol he had always had at home. The custom-built wine fridges, including the spare in the garage. The art deco drinks cabinet that was always opened after a dinner party, offering every spirit known to man, the bottles sparkling prettily against the mirrored interior. The cute little trolly that Sam had bought, loving the way it rattled when she wheeled it around the table to serve her guests. She had left weeks before, screaming with resentment about her life as a captive entertainer, but she had been extraordinarily good at it. And here was Renata, straining to find an old bottle of port or sherry that she could offer her unexpected guests.

"Ah! Look what I have." Her face broke into a smile as she brought a brown bottle to both men, a faded etching of a tall ship on the label. Neither man looked at the bottle. Renata looked so radiant in that moment, smiling wider than Mick had ever seen, proudly presenting the bottle to both of them. Mick took in the delicate dual scoops of her collar bones, the velvety glow of her chest, her defined and sculpted shoulders in her summery dress. She was breathtaking.

"This is Madeira." She stood the bottle before them and twisted around again to find three glasses. She was moving fast now, with excitement. "I don't suppose either one of you knows where Madeira is?"

"It's right there, in that bottle." Lou turned to Mick. "Was that a trick question?"

Mick groaned. "Mate, Madeira is a place in Portugal."

"Yes! *Correto*. It's actually an island off the coast of Portugal. It has belonged to Portugal for around five hundred years. My grandmother was from there. You might not know this, but the British evacuated many of their citizens from Gibraltar to Madeira during the Second World War to keep them safe from the Germans. The Nazis wanted control of Gibraltar to have access to the Mediterranean."

Lou squinted, trying to keep up with this unexpected history lesson.

Renata continued. "My grandfather was one of those evacuees. He was a Spaniard but a complete Anglophile, loved everything British. He went to Madeira and fell in love with my *vovó*."

"Vovo? Like Iced Vovo biscuits?"

"Shut up, Lou."

Renata only laughed. She had become beautifully alive in the telling of her history. "My *vovó*, my grandmother. After the war, they moved over to Lisbon but my grandfather never stopped talking about Gibraltar and how much he respected and admired the British. It's why he gave the blessing to my parents to move out here when I was young and they were struggling to find work. He thought any country which was a part of the British Empire could not be bad."

She had filled the three glasses now with the syrupy, caramel-coloured wine. They held their glasses aloft for a toast.

"Cheers!"

"*Saúde.*"

The tiny glasses looked out of place in the large hands of these two men who sipped with curiosity through pursed lips. Madeira was not their usual tipple of choice. Renata sipped and sighed, still in a reverie about her past.

"I remember you at school," Mick told her.

"I am surprised you do. I pretty much holed up in the library for the last few years of school and you were always playing sport. You only hung out with the cool kids. Not the *emigrantes* like me."

"Yes, but I did know who you were. I guess I would have liked to have gotten to know you but, as you say, we moved in different circles." The truth was, his eyes had always sought her out. In sixth grade, playing elastics with her other Mediterranean friends in the shade of fig trees, he had not been able to stop staring at her as she jumped and pivoted while her friends clapped and sung in a language he did not know, her dark curls bouncing. In later years, as she became increasingly studious, he would often sit behind her in class and watch her curling her hair around one finger as she frowned with concentration into her textbooks. Periodic table. Lord Byron sonnets.

"You started dating Samantha in our final year. She was our school's netball star, right? You made quite the perfect couple."

Mick thought back on Sam, tall and gangly at that time, with pale skin covered in sandy freckles. They had been a natural match, both being so athletic, but all similarities had ended there. Mick came from an established Bombora family which had already started to collect properties in the exclusive strip by the bay, while Sam lived in a fibro-clad home farther up the highway towards the Lilyvale bridge. Mick's family ate at the yacht club every Sunday night, while Sam ate fish and chips out of soggy newspaper with her family on a picnic rug in the park. His family went to Noosa for a full two weeks every Christmas, while Sam went camping down on the south coast and played cricket on the beach with her cousins, dogs winding between their legs.

In recalling that tall, gentle netballer, Mick remembered now the first time he had brought Sam home for lunch. It was hot, and the first course had been a thick slice of rock melon on a plate with a delicate curl of prosciutto next to it. Sam knew what to do with the prosciutto, but she had stared at the rock melon on the shiny Wedgewood plate with a blank face. She had only ever eaten rock melon with her bare hands, or seen it cubed in fruit salads. She had watched very carefully as Mick's family took their knives and made symmetrical slices into the flesh, then used the knives to scoop along the arc of the skin so that the cubes of rock melon slid free and were ready to pierce neatly with a fork. His heart had melted as he had watched her carefully observe how it was done and then follow suit. She had good survival instincts. He felt suddenly and surprisingly overcome with the realisation of the effort it must have taken for Sam to help him create the joint image of perfection for so many years. Until she could simply not be bothered anymore.

"Perfect couple? No, not really, but I understand that's how we presented to the world. And you know what it's like. Once you start having kids, it's just so easy to get distracted in the day-to-day project management of family life. And on top of that I made sure my life was full of lots of other complicated projects. Real estate. Property development. Charities. I even managed the local footie club for a while." He sighed. "We lost each other a long time ago."

Lou had never heard Mick talk like this, and had certainly never heard him express any kind of vulnerability. This was not the Mick he knew. He looked at Renata, who was considering Mick with soft, shining eyes.

"I don't know what's in this wine of yours, but you need to top up Mick here."

Renata refilled all three glasses.

Lou threw his head back and downed his Madeira in one gulp. "Where's the little boy's room, sweetheart?"

Renata laughed as she watched the large bulk of Lou swaying down the narrow hall towards the door she pointed out. There was nothing little about Lou.

Mick sighed. "So what do we do with Rodney Fuckface? I knew he was hopeless, but I didn't realise until tonight he is criminally neglectful. I can't just sit back and let him keep ignoring the issues we are facing here."

"You need to talk to Guil," said Renata softly.

"And why is that?"

"He's already banded together with some other locals." She waved her hand toward the sliding glass door through which the dual towers of the Glades and Sunrise were visible, TV screens flickering from multiple floors. "They know full well they will be at the front line of any bad storm. They are not waiting for your *Rodney Fuckface* to help them or to tell them what to do. They are already hatching plans."

"What sort of plans?"

"Disaster recovery. He's organised a fleet of Jet Skis and kayaks, maybe some tinnies, and started hoarding petrol that could be used to keep them going for as long as possible after a big storm.

He's particularly worried about all the people who live in all the inlets running into the national park. They are secluded as it is today and could easily be blocked off from escape roads."

Mick raised his eyebrows. "That's very motivated of him. Isn't he still at school?"

"Yes, he's in his final year. If I'm honest I would rather he just focus on the HSC. He's bright, he should not be distracting himself." Renata tapped a finger nervously on the bench in front of her. "His own father was trained to perform rescues and still managed to get PTSD. I really think he's too young to be putting himself on the front line."

"How much time does he have on his hands? Does he have an after-school job?"

"No. School and surf. That's his life. And now this."

"Why don't you bring him over for dinner next week? We can try to get him involved in assessing the outstanding maintenance that the apartment blocks on the coast might need to meet new requirements. I've got all those files from Rhys at the real estate agency, plus I have a pile of documents at home from when John and I started building. Detailed plans and layouts. He and I can cobble a plan together — if you think he would be willing to work with me, that is."

Renata sipped her drink and averted her eyes. Dinner seemed unnecessarily intimate, even if Guil were in tow.

Mick heard the slam of the toilet lid, followed by a flush. "It's not a date, Renata. I know your rule about dating men on *that* side of the peninsula. Besides, you are going to be knee deep in dust going through old files. With your son in the room with us. That has to be okay for you, surely."

Renata knew Guil would not be deterred from his plans, and she had to admit the idea of having someone older to help steer and oversee it all made her much more comfortable. Mick clearly had access to a huge local network and resources that Guil and his friends did not. "Let us know which night and we'll be there. I'll bring a dish too."

Lou emerged from the darkened hall.

"We are going to Mick's this week, Lou. Are you joining us?"

Lou blinked with bewilderment. "What did I miss?"

"Nothing Lou, just say you'll come."

"Folks round here never say no to a party at Mick's! I'll bring whatever grog is left over from the closing party tonight."

Mick turned again to Renata. "Tell Guil to bring his ragtag mob over. This shit is about to get professional." He winked.

As they clinked glasses in agreement, a bewildered Guil pushed through the front door and took in the image of his mother laughing with Mick and Lou in his tiny kitchen. Renata had never had guests to their apartment before.

"Speak of the devil!" boomed Lou. His huge heft shifted unsteadily on his stool as he swivelled towards the door, holding his empty glass aloft.

Guil winced. Lou's face loomed large before him, the broken capillaries on his nose glowing the colour of cheap claret. After a few curt nods to the trio, and an especially pointed stare in the direction of his mother, Guil retreated quickly to his bedroom.

"I don't think he likes me," whispered Mick to Renata.

"I'll bring him around, don't worry."

"Another drink?" bellowed Lou.

Mick intercepted his hand as it reached for the Madeira bottle. "Mate, I think you've hit your limit."

"Yeah, you might be right. Should we head out of here?" Lou's large hands started patting the counter, seeking out his keys. "Mick, you comin'?"

Renata held up the bottle of Madeira and met Mick's eyes. "Stay and finish this with me? There's only a drink or so left. Bad luck to leave so little in the bottle, don't you think?"

Lou was not so tipsy that he didn't catch Mick's expression as he turned towards his friend and began to manoeuvre his thick torso towards the door.

"Yes, yes, I'm going!" Mick held the door open until he could see Lou disappear into the elevator. As he went to pull it shut, Renata was behind him with the bottle and glasses in her hands.

"Let's go up to the rooftop. I don't want to disturb Guil." Renata could well imagine him on the other side of his bedroom door with his ear pressed against the flimsy plywood.

"There's a rooftop you can access here?" He dropped his voice to a whisper, following Renata's lead.

"Yes, nothing fancy, just a place to dry laundry really. I think I am the only one to use it for any other purpose."

She led Mick down the carpeted hall, in the opposite direction from the elevator, until they reached a heavy grey door. Stairs going down to street level disappeared into an echoing, cavernous darkness, with a few steps leading up to the broad expanse of the roof. A moon that was a couple of days away from being full glowed to reveal cracked concrete and a smattering of clothes pegs. They picked their way across the roof, avoiding several wide puddles that reflected the moon's glow. In one corner, a small colony of terracotta pots exploded with herbs next to a weathered table and two foldable chairs. It was to this corner that Renata led Mick, setting the bottle and glasses on a table and filling both their glasses with the last of the Madeira.

Mick settled himself as she plucked a thick sprig of rosemary and inhaled its aroma, stroking it thoughtfully against her upper lip.

"Are these your plants?"

"Yes. The only good thing about living in a house out west was my garden. I bet you have a big one? Garden, I mean?"

Mick thought he detected a slight giggle behind the sprig of rosemary. He considered his home on the other side of the peninsula, only a kilometre or so away as the crow flies. Every blade of grass covered; the lawn had been replaced with a huge sparkling pool — which no one used anymore — encased like a topaz jewel in a vast setting of concrete. He wondered what she would make of it when she came over with Guil and his friends. From the little he knew of her, he guessed she would not be automatically awed by its grandiosity. She would likely find it cold and imposing, lacking soul and colour.

"I'm afraid you won't be overly impressed by my gardening skills." He realised as he said this that he had never met someone harder to impress, nor anyone he had wanted to so badly.

He took her in as she leant against the retaining wall of the rooftop. She had come upstairs barefoot. Her ochre-coloured skirt draped loosely around her legs, which were stretched out before her and crossed at the ankle. Her face was turned towards the onshore breeze that was tugging gently at her auburn curls, and she seemed to be sipping lightly from the saline air through Madeira-stained lips. She shimmered against a backdrop of milky spray rising from the rock pools below, illuminated from above by an almost-there full moon.

He, on the other hand, felt the splintered wood of the weather-worn folding chair poking into his backside and his leather shoes pinching after a long night. He awkwardly nursed his still-throbbing hand in his lap, while sipping slowly from his glass with his good hand. He had never felt more out of his league, more incapable of acting on his desires. His glass was almost empty, and he realised with sadness that that would mean Renata would soon be wrapping up the evening. He placed the glass back on the table with the last sip untouched.

Renata suddenly turned to him. "Why so quiet? You don't like it up here on my rooftop? *Your* rooftop, actually."

"I was just thinking about what a magical place it is up here. And how ironic that I have owned this building for years and didn't know that it offered the best view of Bombora."

"You're sitting down." Renata laughed. "You can't even see the view."

"From where I am sitting the view is stunning."

Renata flicked her hair over one shoulder and turned to face the salty breeze once more, unable to look at Mick's glittering eyes. Her stomach contracted with a deep, primal memory of another set of eyes — dark, not blue — that had tracked her around her home out west, watching her while she prepared dinner or folded clothes in front of the television. Intense eyes that made her want to run out onto the burning concrete of her cul-de-sac and disappear into a red sunset vibrating with screaming cicadas. For more nights than she could remember she had lain curled into the foetal position in her bed cringing at the heat radiating from the body next to her, muscles wound tight like a spring. Although her husband had never actually hurt her, the dull flint of his eyes had turned him into someone unknowable, in her mind capable of anything. Intimacy became unthinkable, and so she embarked on a path of trying to attract as little attention as possible. All the warm, stuffy nights she had worn long pyjamas which she pulled on and off in the bathroom, alone, careful that she would not inadvertently expose herself. She had convinced herself her skin was safer under wraps and kept to herself, and she had told herself she didn't need or want the touch of anyone, ever again.

A solitary flash of coral-coloured lightning licked delicately at the horizon many kilometres out to sea and the wind lifted the light silk of her skirt, causing it to tickle against her legs. As if taking this as an omen, she turned back to face Mick with a suddenly determined expression. She saw that his eyes, his "glittering" eyes, were actually watering.

"Mick! Are you ok? You're not *crying* are you?"

"A bug just flew into my eye." Mick awkwardly dabbed at the right side of his face with the hand that was still bundled into a tea towel, soggy with melted ice cubes. He was perplexed when Renata suddenly and loudly laughed, bending forward at the hips, her white teeth shining in the moonlight. Of course he didn't know she was not laughing at his innocent assault by an insect. Rather, she was laughing with the sudden and unexpected feeling of lightness. The heightened and chronic sense of danger she had been carrying around with her momentarily took leave of her up on this rooftop, coaxed away by the electric air and Mick's baffled, sweet expression. Tomorrow, she might erect her walls once more but tonight she would trust the sphere of stars above her and the heaving sea below, booming as if from a watery orchestra pit under her feet. It was as if a stage had been especially set for her to rehearse a long-forgotten dance, and Mick had been well cast as her innocuous and yielding partner. The muscles in her legs, which just moments before were clenched and rigid, now felt fluid as she made her way over to the table. She thoughtfully placed her empty glass next to Mick's, then positioned herself to stand in front of him.

She lowered herself onto Mick's lap. He felt her strong, warm thighs through the thin fabric of her skirt pressing in from each side as she carefully manoeuvred herself into the narrow space between the arm rests of the chair. All of a sudden, the splinters in his backside from the sun-damaged wood were the last thing on his mind.

She lowered her mouth to his and, ensconced in a cocoon of her soft hair which fell forward over her bare shoulders, their sticky lips met and parted. Mick instinctively lifted both hands into her thick, apple-scented curls, groaning from the stab of pain from his punching hand. She lifted her own left hand to find his injured one and plucked it carefully from her curls to guide it to settle on her waist.

"What happened to not dating guys from around here?" whispered Mick.

Her hand descended towards his belt buckle and he took a sharp intake of breath. He felt her thigh muscles contract as she lifted her weight off him just enough to make room for the workings of her hand. Having achieved her objective, she lifted both hands to his neck and allowed her weight to descend once more, both of them sighing in unison.

"Who said anything about dating? Besides, you are on *my* side of the peninsula now."

CHAPTER 12.
CALM BEFORE THE STORM

The morning sun streamed into Renata's apartment, warming her back through her thin pyjamas as she sat at the kitchen island listening absently to the morning news on the television behind her. The three sticky glasses she had used to serve Madeira the night before were lined up next to the sink. Mick's glass still held a mouthful and as she caught sight of it, she felt a warm blush spring up in her cheeks. She chewed her toast slowly and heard Guil padding from his bedroom into the kitchen.

"Morning."

"Hi."

She sensed he was still irritated with her.

"Want some toast?"

"I can make it."

Once the toaster lever was depressed and the tinny hum of the heating element started up, he turned.

"I thought you hated that guy Mick. You said he was creepy."

"I thought he was a bit at first, yes."

"Since when did you two become so close?"

"I wouldn't call what we are *close*."

"You were doing shots with him and Lou last night. I've never seen you do that with anyone. He was *here* in my home."

"We weren't doing shots. We were drinking Madeira. Very different."

"Whatever."

"It was because of what you have been telling me about the rundown buildings around here and the squatting that I agreed to spend time talking to him. I thought it would be good to make sure he knows that we expect him to do his bit and make sure we are all safe here. He is our landlord, you know."

"You didn't look like you were talking about maintenance last night, Mum."

"What is it you're upset about? That I might have started to make a couple of friends? I can't think of the last time I had one. Might be time."

"I don't trust him. He will probably end up leaving like everyone else. Like all the rich people already have. As always, they can buy themselves out of any problem. Even climate change."

"If he was planning to go, he would have gone already with his wife. She's gone off in a huff because he wouldn't sell up and move. He wants to stay and help the community get better prepared for the next storm. And all the ones that will come after that."

"Oh my god, is that what he told you? I see the way he has been looking at you. He just wants to get you into bed."

"Guil! I can guarantee you that I'm not going to end up in his bed."

This did not technically feel like a lie. Her eyes involuntarily flickered up towards the ceiling. *We were over there, just a few metres above the fridge.*

She threw the last corner of toast into her mouth and crossed her arms over her chest. "I did tell him about your group, as a matter of fact. The one that meets downstairs in the storage room. I thought you might need somewhere more comfortable to meet. And someone to help you organise it all professionally."

"What do you mean?"

"I told him about your plans. He was impressed at your initiative. He thinks he can help you."

"Oh yeah? How?"

"Think about it. He lives over on the bay side. All of his neighbours have kayaks and Jet Skis. Small motor boats. He even said a few people have left recently, without selling, and their boat sheds are still full with stuff you — we — could use. He agrees with you that if the next storm causes even slightly more of a surge than last time, the bridge could be impassable and we might need to reach people by water."

Guil grabbed the piece of bronzed bread as it shot out of the top of the toaster with a ping. The scratching of his knife as he buttered it filled the small kitchen. His silence invited Renata to continue.

"Also, he has money he had been raising for the council that he will now obviously not hand over. You saw what he did to the mayor's face. We can use it for first aid kits, food packages. Fuel for boats."

The scratching of the knife on toast stopped, yet Guil still did not turn around.

"Most importantly, he has the contacts and the knowledge to help on more long-term projects. It can't just be about ad hoc responses to sudden disasters. He is even willing to sit down with you and your group" — *ragtag mob,* were Mick's exact words — "to help prioritise and schedule maintenance for the apartment blocks closest to the shore. In fact, we are all invited to his place tomorrow night to kick things off."

Guil swung around.

"So he wants to take over everything?"

"I wouldn't think about it like that. He wants to help. And if you are serious about protecting everyone here in the long term as well as the short term, you would be wise to take him up on his offer." Renata pushed her empty plate away from herself in irritation. "Don't forget you still have to finish school and you are not getting out of *that*. So it would be good to have him onboard until you have more free time, don't you think?"

Guil turned back silently to his toast.

"Honestly, I thought you would be excited."

"Sshh. Turn that up." Guil gestured towards the television. Renata grabbed the remote control from where it lay next to her elbow and hit the volume button with her thumb. They both swivelled to face the screen on the opposite side of the room. The newsreader, famous for her raspy voice and blonde pixie haircut, was poker-faced as she gave her update with images of muddy swirling water behind her on the screen.

"... and have been left stranded again after days of heavy rainfall. Reports are coming in of entire families sleeping overnight on their roofs waiting for the SES to reach them. Residents are being treated with shock and hypothermia in the town hall and are being warned not to use the tap water, which may have been contaminated with waste from the nearby sewerage plant which was badly damaged during the storm. Meanwhile, meteorologists have warned similar supercell storms could form up and down the coast, given the extreme warm weather and humidity we have been experiencing lately ..."

The video footage now filled the entire screen, showing two men helping a distraught, partially dressed woman from her roof into their rocking tinnie. Under one arm, a kitten's tiny face poked out, hard to spot behind the mottled, quivering flaps of the woman's loose upper arm. The tinnie rocked precariously and the woman collapsed, the kitten cowering on her heaving chest.

Renata spoke through a hand covering her mouth. "Those men are not Emergency Services workers — no vests, no uniform."

"A *tinnie*."

"Yes."

"I told you. We're really on our own!"

When it comes down to it, it seems so. Yes."

"Mum, what's *that*?"

They both squinted at the screen. "Is that a *cow*?"

The camera, still pointed at the shuddering woman and her kitten, suddenly shifted to focus on something floating in the fast-moving water behind them. A large, flat head and two panicked bovine eyes barely clearing the brown water were visible for a few seconds before sweeping out of the camera's viewfinder.

"*Meu Deus!*"

"If the storms are hitting that badly up north they might be down here in a few days."

"How ready are you?"

"Nowhere near ready enough."

Renata took his hands. "Please. Take Mick up on his offer. Let him help you, even if it's just this one time. Use his boats, use his contacts and money. The storm might not even travel this far down the coast, but if it does it would make me feel so much better if you had his support."

Guil thought of the group he had assembled. Helen, whose meticulous note-taking meant their list of to-dos now spread over multiple pages in her notebook and whose age meant her talents could only be focused on administrative tasks. Joe and Ellen, whose hearts were in the right place, but were primarily focused on protecting their own building and shied away from committing to anything outside of that. And Matt, who had more than once cancelled coming to a meeting because it clashed with some of his other hobbies such as improv theatre or jiu jitsu. His surfing crew were more reliable and up for any task given to them, but they needed to be given clear instructions and lacked the creativity to come up with their own plans.

"OK, we can try it for now. But as soon as I have been able to recruit more volunteers and have them in good shape, Mick can go back to bullying the council and throwing parties."

. . . .

Guil put the word out and his "ragtag mob" arrived at Mick's by foot or bike. Renata and Helen, the owner of Renata's favourite home on the Esplanade, walked over together, bringing up the rear. Renata carried a wicker basket which she had filled with Portuguese treats: *bifana, bolinhos de bacalhau, pão com chouriço.* The fresh smells of pastry and fried fish wafted up to both women as they took their time, enjoying an intensely amber sunset over a barely moving ocean.

"Hard to believe it's chaos up north. The ocean here is like glass."

"I bet you see some stunning sunsets from your front porch."

Helen signed. "Oh yes. Although the sunrises are better, obviously, facing east as we do. My husband and I were always early risers. We used to sit on the porch together in the few minutes leading up to the sun breaking over the horizon. It was always the same; you would hear birds twittering softly, then they would go suddenly quiet. So strange and wonderful how they know. Only at the exact time that the sun popped up would all the birds, including some bloody annoying kookaburras, explode again with noise. That was the signal for one of us to go inside and start brewing tea."

"Did you always live here? I mean, while you were married?"

"Yes. I am not going to tell you what my husband and I paid for that house back in the fifties. People get angry when I tell them, it sounds like such little money compared to the ridiculous prices today. But we had to scrimp and save to get a foot in, trust me. My husband, Dennis, was a very disciplined and careful man. Thank God. I was so lucky to be his wife."

Renata felt a twist in her stomach, a small goldfish giving a sudden flap.

Helen continued. "We raised three little girls in that house. They could walk to the school and to their ballet class as well. It was heaven back then. So safe, so peaceful. We didn't lock doors, and the kids came and went. They just had to be home when the street lights came on."

"And now? Guil told me you have squatters next to you. Does that make you feel unsafe?"

"Goodness, no! Those young men are wonderful. They have been helping me make sandbags for the front of my house. They are all stacked out the back ready, and they have promised they'll help me set them up if we hear of the next big storm coming in. You saw that I have no garden wall, just a flimsy wooden fence. I've had so much salt water wash halfway up my lawn the last couple of years that all my hydrangeas have died. The boys tell me I should plant cacti. Thrive in salt, apparently."

"And you haven't thought of moving?"

"Where would I move to? The ridiculous thing is that my home is apparently uninsurable. So who would buy it? No one wants to spend money on something they can't protect. I haven't had a policy for a couple of years now. Which is why I am so grateful to those squatters living next to me. They are my only insurance against the next big surge. My girls have all moved away with their families. Besides, I can't imagine living anywhere else. It's where I spent my life with Dennis."

The feeling again. Not as flippant as jealousy, Renata realised. More like a deep grief that wanted to bubble up and be named. She would never know this peaceful, reassuring feeling of a life well lived with a partner whose love endured beyond death. She could not, however, begrudge Helen for having found it. Sweet Helen, smelling of lily of the valley hand cream and Preen iron spray.

The two women linked arms and continued slowly around the point until they reached the bleached stone driveway of Mick's home. Although Renata had never been there, she and Guil had looked it up on Google Maps and she recognised the spiky foliage lining the drive all the way down to a double door in slate grey. The drive was cluttered with bikes and a couple of surfboards leaned against the wall; the ragtag mob was already here.

On pushing open the door, they could hear a high-speed blender whirring and laughter coming from the end of a beige-carpeted hall. They found Lou at the large marble slab of a kitchen island with a slew of fruit spread in front of him. "Daiquiris!"

Behind him was a living room larger than Renata had ever seen. She faced a wall of windows glowing rose gold, throwing everyone in the room into sharp silhouette. Guil and a few of his surfer friends were slumped on the boxy, long sofas lining two walls, and a good few more were cross-legged on the floor. Joe and Ellen perched on the chairs of the dining suite, and Matt appeared to be a no-show.

The room was exclusively designed in a coffee-coloured palette — espresso, latte, flat white. The rug was a slightly lighter shade than the plush carpet beneath it, leading Renata to ponder what its exact purpose was. Where she came from, rugs were a riot of colour designed to break up the monotony of pale walls and bare, wooden or tile floors. Only one defiant jade green vase sparkled on a low coffee table that was covered in small bowls of wasabi nuts and chips. Renata suddenly felt embarrassed at the thought of Mick perched on her creaky bar stools in her tiny flat. It might belong to him, but it was a far cry from his spacious, if bland, home.

Mick bustled in with a few beer bottles in his hands, his eyes seeking out Renata's surreptitiously. The two exchanged polite smiles.

"Gentlemen, make room up here for the ladies please." He swiped at a trio of Guil's friends who were almost horizontal on one of the sofas. They slunk to the carpet and reached up for their beers, while Renata and Helen seated themselves. Renata had never felt more gently hugged by a sofa in all her life. She arranged her Portuguese snacks on napkins on the coffee table and sat back, straight and alert, waiting to see what would happen.

"So everyone, welcome. I'm not exactly sure how these meetings typically proceed but I am here to help. Guil, why don't you take it away?"

Next to Renata, Helen rustled in her hessian shoulder bag and pulled out her well-worn notepad and pen. She cleared her throat. "Actually, I usually kick things off by reading out the last action items."

"Oh, please. Be my guest."

Guil glared at Mick, who resolved to stop talking for the time being.

"So. Let's start with the fuel collection progress. Guil, you were going to look for a storage area for us."

Helen led the group through the minutes and action items from the last meeting, Mick and Renata staying mostly silent and Lou popping in occasionally to pour refills of candy-coloured daiquiri. When they were done, Guil shrugged his shoulders and looked at Mick a little indecisively.

"And that's kind of where we are," he announced.

"It's a great start. But if I can make a suggestion, I think what we need to do before anything else is an audit."

"What kind of audit?"

"Almost like a mini-census. As you already pointed out, there are many people living very close to the water's edge along the inlets we have here. Some are recluse. I personally know of an oyster farmer I used to drive my boat to on a Sunday morning. I haven't been for a while, and I don't know if he is still there. And I am sure there are many like him. I think we need to take stock of how many people there are who would struggle to get away if the waters suddenly rose."

Helen nodded. "True. We should focus on those vulnerable people."

"I suggest we split into groups and take some boats around, meeting people and performing some sort of a risk assessment. We need to know who to evacuate first as soon as we recognise there will be a significant water surge."

"What sort of things should we look for?" asked Guil.

"First of all, assess the age and health of the people you come across. We almost need to triage them. Then check out their homes. Does everything look secure? Think not only of water, but of what would happen in a strong wind. Some of these people live in simple homes with loose corrugated roofs or sheds. We don't want those coming loose and flying around in a tempest. I met a man who lost an arm that way in the Darwin cyclone of '74. Piece of flying corrugated iron sliced it right off under the shoulder."

Mick continued. "Also, ask people what precautions they have thought of themselves and how easily they could do a land retreat. How close are they to well-sealed roads, for example. Find out how many still drive. And, check for animals. People in emergencies can be stubborn and refuse to leave without their furry friends."

Guil remembered the cow he had seen on the news the day before; the wide, panicked eyes straining to stay above the water level. The exhausted, t-shirt clad woman with the tiny kitten almost being crushed under her arm. These were all things he had not thought of.

"I think this census is a great job you young blokes can start with, while I start assessing the priority maintenance needed at the Glades and Sunrise. Guil, these are the two buildings you are most concerned about, correct?"

Mick was making a huge effort to defer to Guil, and it seemed to be working. Guil's demeanour was less hostile than it had been at the beginning of the meeting, although that could have had something to do with the couple of daiquiris he had consumed.

"You can also take some first aid kits with you and drop them off. And maybe some chlorine dioxide tablets in case they need to decontaminate water for drinking in an emergency. Why don't I try to get a stack of those things here tomorrow and you guys can head out in the afternoon for the first audit. Renata, perhaps you want to stay and help me go through all those files? I picked them up from Rhys at the real estate office earlier today."

Guil's eyes flashed at his mother across the room. Renata evaded his glance and brushed some pastry crumbs neatly off the coffee table in front of her. At that precise moment, the front doorbell chimed.

"That must be the pizza!" boomed Lou from the kitchen. "Mick, can you get that?"

Mick jogged down the plush, beige carpet of the hall to the front door and swung it open.

There on the broad black doormat, looking perplexed at the tangle of bikes in the driveway and the sound of a party coming down the hall, stood Sam.

CHAPTER 13. FRICTION

"Why did you ring? You have keys."

"I felt it only fair to warn you I was here. I have no idea what you are up to in there!" Sam forced a laugh in an effort to portray breeziness, but Mick could tell she was nervous. He had to admit she looked good. Her face was scrubbed clean and even with no make-up her complexion looked smooth and clear. Her hair was pulled back into a no-nonsense ponytail and all the blonde streaks had been toned down to her natural brown. Her hazel eyes were clear and focused. She was wearing a soft grey shirt over blue jeans and even her toenails, which were previously religiously shellacked, were clean and natural.

Mick noticed she had no luggage with her, just a small leather slouch bag over one shoulder.

"May I?" she asked.

"It's still your home, Sam."

Sam kicked off her shoes at the door and felt the familiar thick carpet under her feet as she padded towards the kitchen. *How ridiculous to carpet a home on the coast of Australia,* she thought. *All those hours vacuuming sand out of it that I will never get back.*

She took in the sight of Lou filling up the space of her kitchen with his sweaty bulk.

"You!" She laughed.

"Sam?" Lou squinted at her. The last time he had seen her she had been leaning heavily on the arm of a girlfriend as they left yet another long lunch at Vaga, one breast dangerously close to escaping the low cut of her floral sundress. He did not think he had ever seen her in jeans and took a few seconds taking her in. Straight posture, straighter gaze.

"You look good, Sam. Drink?"

"No thanks. Maybe a water."

Both men tried not to show surprise.

"So what's the occasion?" She peeked through to her living room filled with lounging bodies and her eyes went straight to Renata, who was staring back at her with a curious expression. Sam took in her olive skin and thick coils of dark hair. She was as striking as she had been told, rumours having reached her even in Tasmania.

"Where do I even start?" sighed Mick. Sam had only been gone for a few weeks but it felt like the whole world had tipped on its axis. Nothing was the same.

Lou, feeling he was the proverbial third wheel, tiptoed out of the kitchen as quietly as a man of such size ever could, pulling the door to a half-way closed position behind him. The rowdy discussions going on in the living room became more muted as Sam and Mick regarded each other.

"Can I jump right in and ask where you have been? I have been a bit worried."

"I know, and I'm sorry about that. We both needed space."

"You've been with John and Nat, haven't you?"

"I spent the first week or so with them, yes. I couldn't stand any more than that."

Mick's eyebrows became question marks.

"On one hand, I had John in my ear constantly about you. Telling me details about your business together, trying to win me over in the hope I would be able to influence you to accept his offer to buy him out of his share of your portfolio. No matter how many times I told him I was not interested in getting into the middle of all this, he went on and on. I started dreading going to the dinner table at night.

"Then, on the other hand, Nat was at me all day long about how to decorate the house they have found. Should the cabana be Balinese-themed or Tuscan? What colour splashback in the kitchen? She also dragged me around meeting some of her new friends. Same old, same old. The same conversations I have had a million times, just without the ocean view. I started going for longer and longer walks every day by myself. I could reach the town nearest to them in about ninety minutes of walking. I started counting steps. It has felt so good to get moving again."

"That explains why you look so fit. You look really good, Sam."

Sam dipped her eyes. Without make-up, Mick could see the smattering of soft freckles across her face and a light blush springing up underneath them.

"After a week, I left. Haven't the kids told you any of this?"

"They gave me some brief details. Ethan was saying something about … bees?"

Sam laughed. "You are not going to believe this. You remember my cousin Jay? He moved to Tasmania just after we got married. He's always been the hippie of the family. I was wondering where I could go next; I wasn't ready to come back here and John and Nat were driving me mad. I had gone to them to calm down and they were just winding me up more and more. I reached out to Jay and he said of course I could go and stay with them. So I thought, what the hell. I'll go to Tasmania. I've been there for the last two weeks."

"But the bees?"

"Well Jay married a lady from Russia, and she introduced him to something her grandparents used to do. It's bee therapy."

Mick remembered Adele's barely contained anger in their last conversation, accusing Mick of never properly supporting Sam. "Bee therapy, eh? What's that all about?"

Sam looked suspicious. "You really want to know?" Mick nodded, and she took a breath. "When bees make honey, they fan their wings at a very specific frequency to evaporate the moisture from the hive cells and allow the honey to mature. In Russia, it was common practice to put the bee hives in wooden boxes with ventilation holes on top, and then lay a thin sheet over them. You sleep right on top of the bees while they are making honey! You get a vibro-massage from them."

"And the point of that is?" He realised that this may have sounded judgmental, and quickly tried again. "I mean, what would be the benefit of that?"

"Well I could probably try to explain the medical side of it, about how it works on your nervous and circulatory system. Jay and Yulya explained it all to me. But the summary of it is this: it calmed me the fuck down."

"I can see that it worked."

Sam searched Mick's tone for accusation or ridicule. All she could hear was soft concern.

"I know to you it must sound like woo-woo, like I am grasping at straws. All I can say is that staying with Jay did me so much good, and not just because of the bees. I only slept on top of them a couple of times, by the way. The best part was just sitting with him after dinner at night and talking about when we were kids — him, his sister Louise and me. I had completely blocked those years from my memory; it's like the present got so messy and complicated that it took up all my thoughts. I haven't really loved who I have become and it took him to remind me who I was and the potential and excitement I once felt about life.

"He pulled out photo albums. I had not looked at a photo of myself as a teenager for years. I was always in a tree, or on a horse, or building a cubby house in the national park. I was always smiling. I was always *doing* something."

"I remember that girl. I married her, remember?"

"Do you miss her as much as I do? I don't know when it happened, but we reached a point in our marriage where I wasn't required to *do* anything anymore. I had pushed out the babies, built a home. Our first home, I mean. Not this one." She waved her hand vaguely into the cavernous space of the kitchen. "When we built this house, I wasn't even required to do anything. Just look at some colour swatches and pick some furniture, although they only let me pick neutral. Isn't that ironic — all the colour from my life gone. My only job was to blend in."

"I thought you were as excited as I was, Sam."

"Of course I was happy with our — your — financial success. But I wasn't prepared for the loneliness of it. I have been so ridiculously lonely. The kids stopped needing me pretty soon after we renovated here and I felt like I had two choices — sit here alone all day and clean every room on rotation, or get out there and be social. You said that was something I could do to be helpful — stay close to the wives of your business contacts. And so that's what I did. Before I knew it, I was drinking pretty much every day — starting at lunch — and then continuing here at night with you. On the nights you came home, that is."

It was Mick's turn to search Sam's tone for accusation. He wondered how much John had shared with Sam in an attempt to recruit him to his side of the battle.

"But enough about me. We are going to need to find time to get more into this, when we are both ready. What's going on here? Aren't you needed in the living room? It all looks very official."

"Well I have well and truly burned my bridges with the local council and to be honest, I have lost any confidence that they can help us deal with the constant storms that we keep being hit with. So many people are sitting around in uninsured homes and having panic attacks every time it rains. Everyone you see in our living room is here to devise our own contingency plans. Did you see the news this morning? The conditions right now are ideal for brewing the perfect storm. Hotter and more humid than normal."

"I did hear what you did to Rodney. He deserved it."

"Ah, I see you are still well informed."

"I hear everything, whether I want to or not. I have even heard about you and that girl we used to go to school with. Is that her in there? The attractive lady on the couch?"

"Renata."

"Yes. Renata. Shy girl, wasn't she?"

Actually not very shy at all, thought Mick, looking warily at Sam.

"Don't worry, Mick. I don't assume anything about us or how it goes forward. I take a lot of responsibility for what has happened between us and I never want to feel that level of loneliness and resentment again. I just want to see the kids, see my Mum. Tomorrow will take care of itself."

"So you are not going to stay here?"

"No, I rented an Airbnb right near Mum. I like being able to walk to see her and have a coffee with her every morning. She's lost some mobility, even in the few weeks I've been gone."

"Sam, that's a bit weird. You live here. We have a guest room, why don't you sleep in there at least?"

"Are you worried about *how it will look*? That horse has already bolted. Everyone knows I disappeared for a few weeks and assumed we had a huge blowout. You have no idea how many inquisitive calls and messages I have received — and ignored. I actually couldn't care less about what anyone thinks right now."

"I am less concerned about how it looks than I am about you. This is your home and I really do want to find time to talk to you properly. I know that that hasn't been one of my strong suits. I want to work on that."

"It will just be for a while, Mick. I need more space. And it seems like you have your hands full. But if you need help with whatever you are doing in there," she nodded towards the living room, "I have some time. Maybe the kids want to come and help too?" Sam wanted to get to know Renata and joining in with their effort would be a perfect way to do that.

"Well, more hands would be good. Tell them to be here tomorrow afternoon. That's when the Bombora flotilla is going to hit the seas and deliver supplies and medical packages to the more remote homes around here. Adele and Ethan can go with them."

CHAPTER 14. GUEST

It was a strange feeling for Sam, showing up the next day as if she were a guest in her own home. She walked down the driveway past each single plant she herself had pushed into the ground as a sapling or shoot. She had picked up Adele and Ethan from the train station on the way through and the three of them paused at the front door and regarded each other.

"For fuck's sakes, Mum, it's still our house!" Ethan thrust his fist into his pocket and pulled out his set of keys. He pushed the heavy grey door inwards and marched defiantly down the hall.

"Stop! Shoes!"

He backtracked and kicked off his shoes, muttering under his breath.

"Why are you so irritated? I thought you wanted to come and help."

"I actually want to make sure that that bunch of feral surfers don't fuck up my boards and the Jet Ski."

"Shhh, they might be here already."

The three padded together down the hall, finding Mick and Renata in the living room. The furniture had been pushed back against the walls and the pair of them were standing with hands on hips, proudly surveying the neat piles of items they had industriously sorted over the expanse of carpet. Sam felt a low squeeze in her belly at the sight of their sparkling eyes and the evidence of a long task completed successfully together in her living room. They must have been here for hours.

She affected what she hoped was a cheerful and breezy tone. "Wow, you've been busy! Are you hungry? I bought some rolls from the bakery." She lifted a large paper bag up into the air, giving it a little shake and feeling utterly useless. She wondered if Mick was planning to introduce her formally to Renata, who stood barefoot in a pair of denim cut-offs and a loose black t-shirt she had grabbed from Guil's fresh laundry pile.

Mick was utterly absorbed in reviewing his piles of supplies on the floor and left the two women to awkwardly regard each other. Sam realised she did not need a formal introduction; she had also gone to school with Renata, although they had literally never exchanged a word.

"I'd love a roll, thank you," said Renata. "There's fresh coffee in the kitchen too, if you'd like some. And some Portuguese tarts I made."

Adele and Ethan watched wide eyed at the careful dance of these two women graciously offering each other refreshments. Adele poked Ethan in the ribs and whispered, "I would not have missed this for the world."

"Portuguese tarts!" snickered Ethan. "I think Dad likes those."

Mick boomed at them from across the room. "You two! I have jobs for you both. The rest of the group is not coming for a couple of hours but we still have heaps to do to get ready. Ethan, I need you to make maps of the inlets between here and the national park. Laminate them, please. And Adele, you can work with Renata on the first aid kits we want to distribute."

In the kitchen, Sam extracted a chopping board from a drawer and shook some glossy tomatoes from her shoulder bag.

"Nothing like fresh tomato rolls!"

Renata tipped some coffee from a large silver Moka pot into a mug and pushed it over the counter towards Sam.

"I've never seen that thing before. We usually use the coffee percolator."

"Oh, I hope you don't mind. I brought this from home. I think it makes better coffee."

"Does Mick think that too?" Sam could feel that her grin was a little maniacal as she sliced right through the centre of a fat tomato, fleshy white seeds spilling in a juicy puddle over the board.

Renata thought so long about what she could possibly say in reply that the moment passed and she realised it must have appeared that she had simply ignored the question. She knew that she could come across aloof and maybe even a little hostile. She did not want to start off this way with Sam; she was pleasantly surprised at how similar she still was to the tall, gentle netballer she remembered from school. Nothing at all like the woman who had been whispered about at the Vaga farewell party — loud, brash, domineering and almost always drunk. This Sam was poised and even if a little wary (which Renata could understand) had an open expression and kind hazel eyes.

Renata helped Sam arrange the tomato rolls on a platter and watched her carry it into the living room, following closely behind. Adele was squatting and examining the pile of first aid kit items, and Ethan was drawing a simplified map of the bay's many inlets on a sheet of A4 paper, a laptop open in front of him for reference. He gave each map a personalised flourish; here, a breaching whale, there a tiny colony of penguins sunbaking on a sandbar.

The doorbell rang and Mick jogged to answer it, returning with a pile of wooden sticks a few metres long.

"We need to mark these with around ten- or twenty-centimetre intervals. The people we visit today should stick these into the ground and we'll have to tell them to call us when the water gets too high. We'll have to be explicit about which marking they need to start getting concerned about."

"Dad, those sticks are too short. We would have to stick at least half their length into the ground, leaving about a metre or so above. A storm surge is likely to go much higher than that, especially if it's coming at the same time as a high tide. We would be better off just telling them to get ready to evacuate once the water is halfway up to the window, or something as easily understandable as that."

Mick tossed the sticks in the corner in irritation. Ethan was right.

"I'm starting to panic and not thinking straight. That storm cell from up north has not gone right out to sea. I just have a terrible feeling something is going to happen before we are ready. Why are we still so goddamned unprepared?" He sank to his haunches with his head in his hands. Renata and Sam both instinctively moved towards him in concern, retreating equally as quickly when they saw that they were acting in unison.

"*Fark*, did you see that?" whispered Ethan to Adele.

Renata took a step back, making a point of not looking at Mick, and started to tug at a loose thread on Guil's oversized t-shirt.

Finally Sam spoke crisply. "Progress not perfection. Every small step we take is a good thing. Get up, Mick, we need to keep going."

CHAPTER 15. SCAR

At close to high tide, Mick stood outside on the small jetty surrounded by Guil and his friends. In addition to the tinnie and inflatable boat with an outboard motor that Mick had pulled out of his shed, Ethan had brought an additional two tinnies over from their neighbours' boat sheds.

"Jerry's not at home, Dad, but I am sure he won't mind. He never locks his shed. I'll put it back later. Susie was home and was happy to let me take hers. And she insisted on giving me these." He dropped a tin of Scottish shortbread on the jetty which Mick kicked behind him with an impatient flick of his heel.

"So we have four boats and the Jet Ski."

"*I* am taking the Jet Ski," said Ethan decisively. He made a point of making eye contact with Guil as he said this. Guil stared back in what he hoped came across as perfect indifference.

Mick counted the bodies assembled around him. "So if you are on the Jet Ski, Ethan, then we are one short for one of the boats. I really wanted everyone to be in pairs. It's safer that way."

"What about me?" asked Adele. "Including me there are eight for the boats, not counting Ethan."

"You want to go out too?" asked Sam, looking surprised.

"Of course. Why wouldn't I? I know these waterways as well as anyone here. Probably better."

Sam cast her eyes at the sky. It was still clear. She realised it was a double standard to be concerned about her daughter heading out into the still afternoon. She was used to Ethan being more of a risk taker, whereas Adele had always been more cautious and measured.

Adele chose one of the tinnies and jumped down off the jetty, landing on bent legs and with arms stretched out to steady herself. She sat down and rested a hand on the tiller of the motor and stared up defiantly at Mick, who took her lead and started to herd the young men towards the boats.

"OK, that's two per boat, perfect, we need room for the canned food and bottled water. And the first aid kits."

Renata and Helen helped load up the boats with supplies while Mick answered questions and gave final instructions.

"OK, here are your maps." As Mick handed them out, he indicated to each pair which inlets to focus on. "Please do your drops of food, water and first aid kits but don't force them on anyone — some might be more prepared than others. And just make some notes about each resident, we can create a priority rescue list when you're all back. You've got around three hours till the sun sets."

Sam still looked uneasy about Adele joining the mission. "Shouldn't we mark down which boat is going into which inlets?"

Mick patted his pockets. "I didn't bring a pen, Sam. Honestly I don't think it's necessary." He turned to the pairs bobbing in their small boats. "I want you all out now so that you have enough daylight."

The boats set out with Ethan swooping amongst them on his Jet Ski, like a sheepdog keeping his flock intact. Sam stood with her arms crossed at the end of the jetty, watching intently. When Adele did not turn around and wave, she suddenly swivelled and followed Mick inside.

Helen and Renata, now alone, stood shoulder to shoulder and watched the boats retreat. Even after they had all rounded the first lip of coastline and disappeared into the next bay, the putt of their motors could still be heard.

"It's so still," murmured Renata. "It almost feels like an overreaction to be doing this. Like we are imagining the danger."

"Honey, I can tell you this is not an overreaction and we don't have as much time as we think we do."

"What do you mean?" Renata had just seen her son proudly commandeer one of the tinnies out into the bay and felt a sudden shudder of panic at Helen's tone.

Helen ran a hand over her lower belly. "Both my girls were born via caesarean. The scar is pretty thick and knotty after two goes at it. It itches and throbs when a bad weather cycle is on the way."

"And? Is it throbbing now?"

"Like a bastard."

. . . .

Sam found Mick in the kitchen.

"You're really OK with sending Adele out?"

"Of course, why wouldn't I be? She's the sensible one. Besides, the weather is looking fine for now. It won't take them long to finish their rounds and then they'll be back." When Sam didn't answer he continued. "Why are you so bothered? Why don't you feel the same way about Ethan?"

Sam pulled herself onto a stool and rested her chin in her hands, thinking. Sitting with her thoughts was something she was not very practised at, having always preferred to sedate their chatter. Her cousin Jay had a fridge magnet with the message; *Feelings are like visitors — let them come and go.* She tried to invoke this wisdom now as she felt a wave of foreboding wash over her.

After a few moments she spoke in a low voice. "Ethan put us — and himself — through so much in his teenage years that I feel like I already had to create a bit of healthy detachment. But Adele — well, she has been my absolute rock. I can't explain why I feel so panicked at her leaving with the boys just now. I know she is the pragmatic one, I know she will be the one who will make the right plans if something goes wrong out there. They are lucky to have her."

Mick laughed. "Do I need to remind you of just how sensible she is? I remember once — she couldn't have been more than six or seven — we were having a silly conversation over dinner. She'd just come back from the dentist and I was moaning about the bill. I turned to her and said, 'If I can give you one piece of advice, it's to marry a dentist. You'll never run out of money.' Then you told her, 'Adele, you can also *be* a dentist. That's a better solution.' Do you remember what she said then?"

"*I will just brush my teeth twice every day.*"

Sam laughed. "I had forgotten about that. Yes, she was always very sensible."

"But also a bit of a worrier."

"Has she been worried about me? While I was gone?"

"Not about where you were or if and when you were coming back. More about the state of our relationship and …"

"And?"

"Your drinking. She puts a lot of the blame on me for that, I think."

"She doesn't miss anything, does she?"

"What does that mean? That you blame me too?"

"No one lifts the drink to my lips but me. I have to take accountability for that."

"I hear a *but* coming."

"*But* … I've never had to work very hard to access alcohol, have I? It just appears all around me. I barely empty a bottle and — *boom!* — the next time I go to the fridge, there's another one there. I only had to walk into Vaga, and Lou would pour me a drink. It would be sitting on the table before I had even sat down. Adele has been the only one who has actively challenged me. And she's done it repeatedly over the years. She has just been very careful to do it while you were not around. I think that's why things escalated after she and Ethan moved out. No one was watching out for me anymore."

Mick thought back on the last phone conversation he had had with Adele while Sam was still in Tasmania; her tight voice, and how easy it had been for him to picture the taut, serious expression on her face. It was an expression she had been wearing since she was a little girl.

Sam continued. "Maybe that's why seeing her head off in the boat has rattled me. I try so much harder when she is around."

"That's a hell of a pressure to put on her, Sam. What can *I* do to make things easier for you?"

Sam stared at Mick in surprise. "Let's just get through this storm, if it actually hits. We can talk about ourselves later. I can't discuss it now, with other people around. It's a little distracting." She pointedly turned to stare out of the kitchen window. Mick's gaze followed to where Renata and Helen were standing on the jetty. A sudden brisk wind had picked up and was pulling at Renata's thick ponytail. Helen frowned at the sky as she pulled her cardigan tighter around her torso.

Mick knew exactly who Sam meant by "other people". Any discussion about their future now held a third person in it. He felt grateful that he had at least the duration of the storm to ready himself for it.

. . . .

In order to distract herself from her growing unease, Renata returned to the living room. She could hear the low voices of Mick and Sam coming from the kitchen and wanted nothing more than to leave. When she heard short bursts of laughter — first from Mick, then Sam — it hit her like shrapnel. She felt a dark mood start to come over her.

She looked around the immaculate room, Sam's invisible presence surrounding her. Every piece of furniture, every tasteful piece of art, handpicked by Sam. Renata would never have agreed to bringing Guil and Mick together on this enterprise if she had known Sam would reappear. She felt disgusted at herself, pouncing on Mick while his wife was away. She could not believe she had been so naive; had she really thought Sam would just not show up again? From the chatter at Vaga and Mick's own avoidance of the subject over the last few weeks it had been easy for Renata to discount Sam's existence and even to imagine she might never return to Bombora. Before yesterday, Renata's only image of her had been of a pale schoolgirl in a sea of similar looking girls in matching gingham uniforms, their exact features bleeding into each other like watercolours on canvas. Yet now Sam had reared up, horribly adult and vivid on her own doormat, close enough for Renata to smell her body spray and the underlying sweat it was meant to conceal. Renata saw that her features were far from those bland and generic ones of her memories; although Sam was clearly tired and overwhelmed, Renata could see a feline beauty in her speckled hazel eyes and arched eyebrows and a grace in the way she moved her long limbs through the rooms of her house.

Renata watched her with sad fascination, lowering her eyes if Sam looked over at her. The most horrible realisation of all was her apparent friendliness. Renata absolutely did not want to start to *like* this woman.

As uncomfortable as she was, she was determined to stay until Guil arrived back with the flotilla. She sat before the huge pile of manila folders Mick had gathered, each labelled with the names of his many properties. The Glades, Sunrise, and the building she lived in, the Palisade, along with a handful of commercial properties at Devlin Point. The folders were stuffed with various plans and diagrams, as well as inspection protocols and receipts for maintenance activities. It was a mess. Everything was hopelessly out of order; some documents had no date stamp and indicated their age only through the thickness of the paper and whether there were any folds or stains. This was not going to be easy.

"Just go through and make a prioritised list of what urgent repairs or upgrades need to be done," Mick had advised. "Look for anything that might be relevant to storms or what might need to happen in an evacuation: leaks, lifts that don't work, condition of retaining walls, that sort of thing. Guil has already spoken to me about the electrical panels and lift shafts and what we need to do to waterproof the basement areas."

"And which properties get priority?"

"I agree with Guil that we should focus on the buildings closest to the coast. Start with the Glades and Sunrise. As much as it hurts me to say it, ignore the commercial properties. We should focus on where people actually live."

"Will you even have time to do anything about any issues we find?"

"Whether it's this storm or the next one, these things need to be done regardless. We may as well get it all on the radar now."

Renata was glad of the distraction, emptying the contents of the bulging folders and organising them into smaller piles across the broad expanse of the dining table. She grabbed some Post-It Notes and started labelling, proud of the colour-coded order as it bloomed in front of her.

As the sun dipped, Mick wandered over for a progress report. Her stomach fluttered, and she sat up straighter.

"How's it looking?" She could feel the pull of his gaze and the warmth in his voice. Keeping her eyes down, she assumed a demeanour of cool efficiency.

"I've focused mainly on the Glades and Sunrise like you asked. There have been some issues with the sump pump at Sunrise over the last couple of years and I can't find evidence that it was replaced. I think that needs to be checked quickly. But generally I think the issues are structural. Both have emergency exits that are *below* ground level. That's not going to be helpful if the lifts are not working and people need to exit into a flooded stairwell."

"Or the pressure of the water might even prevent the door from opening," agreed Mick, matching her business-like tone but still trying to meet her skittish eyes. "I will send over one or two of the guys when they are back from the inlets to see if we can somehow sandbag the exits or find another exit plan if we are evacuating. They should probably also ask all the residents to be on notice to move their cars out of the underground parking. Anything else?"

"Well, something about bad roof drainage at the Palisade. Nothing else. But as we keep saying, the Palisade is a lesser priority. I guess that means *I* am a lesser priority." Renata tried to sound flippant as she said this.

Mick answered her softly but emphatically. "*Never.*"

The room suddenly darkened as if someone had drawn thick curtains over the windows and a gust of cold air unsettled one of the piles of paper at the corner of the table. Mick and Renata hastily gathered the piles into an ordered stack, weighed it down with a thick bronze candle holder, and made their way back outside to the jetty. Helen was perched on the edge of the weathered wood, feet swinging beneath her.

"See? My scar never lies."

A dark mass of cloud had reared behind them and was only now passing over the rooftops to their side of the bay. The surface of the water, which had been so still and glassy just a couple of hours ago, was now covered with frenetic caps moving in all directions. The chime of the boats anchored in the bay rang out as they started slowly to rock, nudging each other with hollow sounding knocks.

The trio were silent, straining to hear either the staccato beat of the tinnies' outboard motors or the smooth whir of the Jet Ski.

The first fat drops landed on the dry, warm wooden planks of the jetty.

CHAPTER 16. STORM

Sam peeked through the kitchen window to see Renata still perched on the outdoor settee. Rain sliced down diagonally, battering the deck approximately one metre from her feet and occasionally splattering her long legs which were bare under her denim cut-off shorts. It was impossible to see much past the seething mass of water in the pool, water exploding downwards and upwards simultaneously. The hammering sound of rain was so constant that even the thunder became mere background noise, an occasional punctuation to the roar of water around them. The storm was nowhere near above them yet; the still-languid pattern of lightning strikes revealed that.

Despite many attempts to lure Renata inside into the dry kitchen, she stubbornly refused with a shake of the head. Sam could understand she was worried about Guil; after all, she herself had two children out in this deluge. Yet Renata's refusal to so much as meet her eyes seemed to go beyond anxiety and concern, especially as she could feel Renata's eyes bore into her whenever she turned her back. Sam decided to suspend any kind of reaction until after the storm; they both had plenty of other things to think about right now. As she watched Renata through the glass, she saw her run her arms vigorously over her upper arms and pull her legs under her body.

Sam padded up the stairs to retrieve a couple of soft cashmere throws from her bedroom. She had not been in there for several weeks and stood for a moment with her toes sinking into the flawless cream carpet. The covers on Mick's side of the bed were tossed open, his pillow still bearing the indent from his head. Her side of the bed was pulled taut and straight, pillow geometrically poised above the razor-sharp turn of the quilt (which she found a relief, although *had* someone else slept in her bed they could naturally arrange the covers to conceal that easily enough). A book she had been trying to read for months lay on the side table next to her pillow, dog-eared and abandoned. On top of it was her black lacquered box of aspirin, glimmering in the subdued light. An old life, left behind. She never wanted to be that woman chewing on dry aspirin on a daily basis ever again.

"Here." Sam handed Renata a wrap and sat down next to her, pulling her own wrap tight around her shoulders. The air had cooled by what felt like twenty degrees. She knew that to suggest going inside one more time was futile; Renata had refused to leave her post for the last two hours, even though it was no longer possible to make out the rocky point the boats had rounded on their way out. It was not even possible to see the homes on the opposite side of the bay a mere three hundred metres away, nor the jetty on the other side of the churning swimming pool. An artificial night had descended and the street lights around the bay, on timers, had not yet been activated. The women stared into what seemed to be a dark void. Their eyes registered emptiness, but every single one of their other senses perceived a menacing, pressing wall closing around them on all sides.

This is where Mick found them in anxious silence; Sam and Renata, bonded in maternal worry in matching cashmere wraps.

"Not one of them is answering their phone. They are either sheltering and don't have reception, or they are trying to make it back here and can't take their phones out, or even hear them over this noise."

"Tell me again why we sent them out in such tiny boats with no covers?" asked Sam.

"No one thought the storm would hit so fast. Up until a couple of hours ago the news was reporting that the storm cell had all but disappeared out to sea. I thought today would just be a reconnaissance mission, and the real work would happen tomorrow, if at all."

"They all left in normal street clothes. No one had wet weather gear with them. What do we do? Sit here and wait?"

"What else can we do? Even if I had another boat, which I don't, I would not be able to find them in this rain. There is zero visibility. The best I can do is keep our jetty light on and quickly go and ask the neighbours to keep their lights off so the kids know exactly where to navigate towards."

Renata's eyes did not leave the approximate direction of where the boats should be returning from.

"Can't we call in for help? Or ask a bigger boat to go and look for them?"

"No bigger boat can get into all the small inlets, that's why we sent them in the tinnies in the first place. We can only hope that the rain eases and they manage to get back soon."

"Is there anything we can do in the meantime? Should we be going over to the apartment blocks and seeing how they are holding up?"

Renata was quick to answer. "I am not going *anywhere*." This was the first time she had spoken in almost an hour.

Mick tried to catch her eyes but her head stayed resolutely pointed towards the bay. "That's OK, stay here. I'm going to go and check in on Helen. She wanted to sandbag the front of her place. The boys who had promised to do that for her are out in the boats. But please call me as soon as one of the boats makes it back. "

"You really think the waves could come up that far?" asked Sam.

"Maybe not tonight, but if it storms like this for another day or so the swell could be huge. Vaga was flooded at this time of month, remember? That means we are due another full moon, which could mean another king tide."

"Not so soon, surely? We only used to get king tides a couple of times a year."

"The past is hardly a reliable indicator for what is going on now."

The sound of feet running along the length of the pool caused Renata and Sam to jump up from their seats. Two figures appeared at the top of the stairs, emerging suddenly from the darkness. Guil and Ethan, still bent against the rain, stood panting in their clinging, wet clothes. The clamour of rain had made it impossible to hear the Jet Ski approaching and being secured to the jetty.

Sam sprung up to retrieve towels from inside the house.

"Oh my God, Guil …" Renata hovered around her son anxiously. "Where are the others? Why are you alone?"

Guil leant forward and shook his hair vigorously, then wiped the wet locks behind his ears as he took a deep breath in.

"We had all split up when the storm hit. I have no idea where the others are. Ethan came and found us and brought me back on the Jet Ski. The boat is still back with Dave. It's so full of water; we tried to scoop it out but it was impossible. We have to go and get him — and the others — some other way. Those open boats are useless in this rain."

"Where is he? We can't leave him there overnight!"

Sam reappeared with two beach towels. "We can't leave *any* of them there overnight." She threw one towel to Guil and wrapped the other around Ethan's shoulders. "Where is Adele?"

Ethan shrugged. "Like Guil said, we had all split up when the storm hit. *Fuck* Dad, why didn't we write down which arm each of us went into?"

"Because we didn't think the storm would hit so soon," retorted Mick, more than a little defensive. He felt both women staring at him.

"I have no idea of which arm we were in … Ethan, what was it called?"

"I found you near Beckitt's Beach."

"So what did you find out there?" asked Mick.

"At first it was all pretty standard. We were doing what you asked us to do, just going and speaking to the people there and asking them if they were prepared and if they needed anything from us. Then the rain started, and a family let us hang out on their veranda to wait it out. But as you know, it just hasn't stopped. We couldn't call — no reception."

"So the residents are well prepared? They are all OK?"

"The ones at the waterfront, yes, so far so good. But there are houses way back from the water at the escarpment and they are really copping it."

"How can the rain be worse for them than down at the beach? Aren't they protected back there?"

"Well yes, you would think so, but the water is coming right off the cliff above them and pouring straight down on them. It's like a muddy waterfall."

"Shit, of course. I know why." Mick rubbed his eyes. "The bushfires last summer burned right to the edge of the escarpment there. There is no vegetation left to hold the soil down. The rain must be just sliding right off and over the edge and taking all that soil with it. Soon it won't be just muddy water coming down. It will be thick mud."

Guil nodded. "Dave is helping evacuate the houses from the back to the front. Funny, we thought we were going to help the homes closest to the shoreline. But the reverse is true."

"And if it's happening there at Beckitt's Beach, it must be happening farther along the escarpment as well. Remember how bad the fires were last summer? The national park was destroyed all the way to the ridge for kilometres towards the south."

"We need to get more people over there to help. There are way more people to evacuate than we were expecting. And there are animals, like you said. One woman with two pigs! She won't go without them. Cats and dogs everywhere."

"Why can't they drive out? Why do *you* have to go back?" Renata moved towards Guil as if she would physically prevent him from leaving again.

Mick shook his head. "All the roads in and out lead along the escarpments. If the homes are at risk of mudslides from above, then so are the roads. Getting them out by boat is safer."

The phone rang and Sam disappeared inside.

Ethan finished rubbing himself vigorously and dropped his towel on the settee. "I can't go back out with the Jet Ski to find the others, I need a boat with a strong light and a roof."

"How can we send out more boats into this rain?" asked Renata.

Ethan retorted with irritation. "How can we *not*? My sister is still out there. The other boys are still out there."

Sam reappeared. "That was the nursing home. They want to evacuate the residents. They know they are being cautious at this point, but they can't afford to wait too long because it would be impossible to push that many wheelchairs and beds through even a little bit of water if it comes up over the footpath. Apparently Emergency Services are down there closing off the promenade all the way out towards the Cove."

"That was going to be my next point — we need to get Emergency Services involved. We are literally in over our heads here." Mick thought back to just a few hours earlier. The kids had set out in their tinnies, laughing and calling to each other, feeling purposeful with their laminated maps, orderly piles of supplies and paper bags of sandwiches Helen had prepared for them. There had been the feeling of a summer excursion to it; now they were stranded in some of the many branching fingers of the bay as it reached deeply into the national park, with a swollen bay pressing in on them from behind and a slippery roof of mud becoming more and more unstable above them. Mick thought for a moment. "Why don't we go find the Emergency Services? It will be much faster than calling it in. Their lines must be ringing off the hook right now."

"Mick, someone needs to get Mum!"

"We can do both things together, Sam. Grab your stuff."

"No, I want to stay here till we have heard about Adele!"

Mick was already pulling on a light rain jacket. "I am sure Adele is sheltering from the rain. You may as well keep yourself busy while we wait. Your mum will want to see *your* face before she goes anywhere, you know that."

Renata made her way over to Sam and stood before her. "I won't move from this deck. I promise to call you the minute someone comes back. And I won't stop trying to call Adele."

Flooded with relief that her own son was back out of the storm, she felt nothing but compassion now for Sam whose eyes had started to gleam with panic.

Renata reached out to squeeze her hand. Sam let her.

. . . .

Guil and Ethan headed off on foot to the small marina at the end of the bay in the hope of finding someone who could give them access to more weatherproof boats, or at least point them in the right direction. Mick watched them disappear under a broad umbrella whose shape above them was flattened by the relentless rain.

Leaving Renata alone in the house, Mick and Sam drove down to the northern side of Bombora, a place where the promenade wound down low towards the sand. As they drove eastwards over the slight crest of land towards the beach, a violent wind slammed into the nose of the car. They had not realised how protected they had been over on the bay side; over here, the thick Cook Pines were violently shaking off thick branches that rained down on the streets below. Mick had to work hard to navigate his way through the foliage-riddled street. At one stage, a heavy thud exploded on the car roof above Sam's head, and they were both grateful for the sturdy European-designed car.

Whereas at home the rain had been a solid, uninterrupted deluge, on this side the fierce wind dragged the rain one way, then another, so it swept over and around the car like a wild dance. One minute it was beating at Sam's window, the next it was pounding at them from behind. In the moments that Sam could get a somewhat clear view out of her window, all she could see were blinking streetlights and, far above her, a steady orb of light heading towards the beach.

"Is that a *helicopter?*"

A barricade prevented Mick from being able to approach the nursing home from the beach side. A miserable looking police woman in a bulky black raincoat used her torch to indicate to Mick that he needed to turn left away from the beach. They parked well away from any low hanging trees and ran around to the entrance of The Pines. The helicopter that Sam had seen from the car was being rocked by the erratic winds just in front of them, above the beach. Four of the staff were huddled at the entrance of the home, dragging nervously on cigarettes and watching the helicopter duck and weave. They nodded at Sam.

"What is the chopper for?" she asked them.

"The palm trees lining the promenade. They have been sick for years. Trunk rot. In a wind this strong, they could get pushed backwards and fall on the houses behind them. So they are being ripped out. If they get those done, apparently they want to take away the lifesaving tower, too."

Mick scoffed. "*This* is what the Emergency Services is prioritising right now? Why haven't they dealt with those sick palms before now? Oh you know what, don't bother answering. Rodney Fuckface."

"Where is Mum?" Sam asked a grey faced nurse taking the last anxious drag of her cigarette.

"All packed up and ready to go. Thanks for coming and getting her, we really think it's safer for her with you for the next couple of days."

"Is everyone going?"

"Most, although we do have some residents here with no local families. We've been asked to evacuate who we can, and tomorrow morning, depending on the state of the rain and tides, we may have to ring around and find them hospital beds.

Hopefully this is all just a precaution." As she spoke, foam from the crashing waves on the other side of the footpath extended a few metres up into the dark sky.

"Sam, you go find your mum and get her ready. I am going to see if I can find someone from the Emergency Services down the road. I won't be long." Mick pulled the hood of his raincoat up and over his head and started jogging down the street.

Sam weaved her way down the corridor, usually quite hushed with only a handful of staff ferrying medications and food from room to room, but now full of the elderly residents either being supported to walk or pushed in their wheelchairs towards the front door. Most looked animated and excited, packed into raincoats and sturdy sneakers. Some of them had only worn slippers and robes for months, even years. A queue was forming at the front door as staff with huge umbrellas were shuttling the residents and their carers in small groups towards the back of the building and into the next street, which was the closest place to park. The Emergency Services refused to drop the barricades to allow them to be picked up at the door of the home.

Sam's mother was waiting on her bed, a large sports bag packed next to her.

"*There* you are! Are you taking me back to the little Airbnb you rented?"

"No, you won't be comfortable there. It's barely big enough for me. Ethan is back at the house, and hopefully Adele will be soon, too. You can hang out with the kids while I help Mick and Renata tomorrow with the aftermath of this storm. And," she added somewhat defensively, "it is still *my* home too, you know."

"Who the hell is Renata?"

"So much to tell you, Mum."

They made their way to the front doors, her mother calling out farewells to her fellow residents as each one was ferried off into the night, anxious relatives holding umbrellas and rain-coats over them. The nursing home had run out of wheelchairs by this stage; some of the elderly needed to be carried, too frail to manage the slippery footpaths. One of the dementia patients whooped with excitement to be leaving the home, lifting her face to the streaming rain. "Oooooh!" She laughed, opening her mouth and feeling the unexpected harsh sting of rain needle her tongue.

Gutters were starting to overflow and spit dirty, foamy water back over the pavements, mixing with the relentless rain. Everyone who was not already wearing shorts rolled their trouser legs up their shins before hurrying off into the sodden night, most barefoot in order to grip the submerged pavements even better. Sam peered down the street towards the flashing lights of the Emergency Services, willing Mick to return quickly. She could feel her mother's thin shoulders tremble under her thin rain coat, and she was also desperate to get back home and see if Adele had made it back safely. She did not want to launch into an explanation right now to her mother about the ill-timed flotilla that she and Mick had sent out into the bay a few hours earlier. It all seemed ridiculously naive now. The old Sam would have screamed at Mick for this unfolding of events; now, she reluctantly accepted joint responsibility for what had transpired. She would stand shoulder to shoulder with Mick — and Renata — until all four boats of the flotilla were back home safely.

. . . .

They arrived back at the house to find Renata still alone on the back deck. No boats had arrived. Renata simply met Sam's eyes and shook her head glumly, holding her phone in her hand.

Sam swallowed her panic and helped her mother upstairs to the guest bedroom. Barb stroked the bronze quilted bed cover. "Fancy. It's nice to be on a real bed. One without wheels."

"Maybe I'll crash in here tonight with you. Girls' sleepover! Won't that be fun?"

"Darling, what's going on? *Your* bedroom is at the end of this hall."

"Mick and I haven't had a chance to talk yet. I don't see that happening till this storm has passed. I need to be patient."

"It sounds like resolution might be what you are looking for?"

"Maybe. I'm not closed to the idea. But I suspect he has eyes for someone else."

"This Renata? Is that the lady downstairs?"

"Yes. Funnily enough, she was in our class at school but we weren't close. She apparently moved away for a long time and came back recently after she lost her husband. She and Mick have been spending a lot of time together. I think he's smitten."

"Smitten doesn't always last, love."

Sam shrugged. That all seemed a lot less important right now than getting Adele back safely.

"Why is she even here?" asked Barb.

Before she could fill Barb in on the reconnaissance mission that had gone awry, she heard yelling from downstairs.

"Sam! A boat is coming!"

Downstairs, Mick was standing at the top of the stairs leading down to the pool which had filled to within a centimetre of its tiled upper lip and continued to be pummelled by rain from above.

"It's coming from the wrong direction!"

They watched as a small cuddy outboard pulled up to the jetty. A hunched figure jumped out and quickly tied on, and helped someone else out of the cabin as the boat bobbed erratically up and down. They ran past the pool, bounded up the stairs, and stood panting and smiling at the assembled group.

"We got one!" declared Guil.

"Well don't get too relaxed, we need to head out again. Well done, both of you."

Renata spun to face Mick. "Wait a second. All you asked them to do was get a boat. Which they did. It's time for the adults to take over now. I don't want Guil going out again!"

"I'm sorry, Renata, but I do need to take both Ethan and Guil with me. Only they know where the other boats were last seen and we have no idea how much work there is to do and how many people we might need to bring over here. After this much rain, I would be surprised if that mud hasn't come down yet."

Renata turned to Guil. "Please, you don't have to go. You've done enough. Mick, I thought you were going to organise the Emergency Services to take over. If you choose to go, that's on you. But you can't take Guil."

"I did speak to them down at Bombora. They are aware of the situation and said they would try to send a rescue boat around sometime tonight. I'm not holding my breath; I am sure they will stick to the beachfront for most of the night. That's where all the bigger tax payers live," he muttered sardonically.

Mick turned to Sam. "You'll need to keep an eye out for them just in case. If they do come, give them one of the maps Ethan made. I told the kids to concentrate on the larger inlets, if that helps."

Guil turned to his mother whose eyes were shining with fear. Only he knew the memories that were being stirred by the howling wind and talk of Emergency Services. She had seen his father head off to a seemingly routine emergency operation without a second thought, only to be transformed by some cruel alchemy of wind and water into a moody and volatile husband and father. If that could happen to a man with thorough training and years of experience, what could happen to her son?

"I know this is hard for you, Mum. But you know I can't leave Dave out there. I promised him I would go back. And the others — I roped them all into this operation, remember? My ragtag mob."

Mick looked sheepish. He had never expected Renata to reveal the flippant name he had created for them. It seemed an incredibly cruel name now, given they were all scattered and totally unprepared in this wild squall, and for one reason only: he, the adult, had sent them out there.

Mick cleared his throat. "I take full responsibility for sending you all out. And I wish I could get the rest back by myself but I need help to find them." He turned to Renata and lifted one of her hands from Guil's shoulder. "I need you to go and check in on Helen as soon as you can make it over. I was supposed to help her out with the sandbags, but the nursing home situation distracted me. Please make sure she is OK? And I'll see you back here tomorrow." Sam averted her eyes while Mick continued to clasp Renata's hand inside both of his. "Please rest up. Tomorrow will be an even bigger day. Thank you for everything you've done."

Gently he dropped her hand and made his way to Sam, feeling like a horrible cliche of a two-timer. He was full of self-loathing at putting both women through this awkward situation. He never imagined they would ever be in the same room together, let alone sharing the horror of these unfolding events, and now having to watch the painful theatre of his dual farewell and dispensing of assurances. He felt Renata's eyes acutely observing as he lightly kissed Sam on the cheek. "I *will* bring Adele back. Please trust me."

As much as the churning bay filled him with apprehension, he couldn't wait to be off this deck and away from the two sets of eyes measuring his every move. He nodded to Ethan and Guil. The three pulled their hoods over their heads, jogged into the rain and boarded the bobbing boat, leaving Renata and Sam to watch their slow progress through the curtains of rain over the bay.

Once again, the two women stood in matching cashmere wraps, sharing their anxiety in silence. The only thing that mattered was the safe return of their children; anything else was suddenly a mere triviality.

CHAPTER 17. RESCUE

Mick pointed the bow of the boat directly into the incoming waves and pushed his way forward towards the mouth of the bay, bracing himself against the turbulent rise and fall of the boat. Ethan stood next to him, holding one of his laminated maps and illuminating it with his headlamp. Guil was staying dry downstairs in the cabin, his face pressed against a window and keeping an eye out for any tinnies tied up against the shore.

"Turn in here." Ethan pointed towards an inlet that forked off to the right. Mick carefully navigated around a large boulder and dropped the revs of the motor, straining to see land on either side of him. As they continued deeper into the inlet, the few, dark houses gave way to long stretches of bush and the occasional narrow strip of sand, the water surge already covering most of the beaches that Mick knew well. This inlet had been a popular place for his family to come for picnics when the children were small.

"Is that someone waving?"

As the volume of swollen water underneath them caused the boat to bob and keel, the two men peered into the darkness. A thin figure draped in a long rain poncho stood in a star shape, arms stretched upwards.

"I think it's Adele!"

The boat came as close to the figure as they could manage.

"Dad! Dad! Is that you?" Ethan and Mick both shared the same relieved exhale as Adele's voice carried over to them.

"I can't stop here, where can I tie the boat on? Where is the nearest jetty?"

"Keep going a bit farther, there's one coming up." Adele ran alongside the boat, occasionally disappearing behind clusters of bush and then reappearing in her flapping plastic, yelling encouragement.

"Here! Here!"

It was not easy to align the boat to the jetty and pull in, the wind and swirling water causing the boat to rock precariously. Adele grabbed the rope that Mick tossed over to her and quickly secured it to a wooden pillar.

Mick jumped across onto the jetty, the water level so high that the wooden slats were actually lower than the boat deck. Ethan quietly followed, and the two men enclosed Adele in an embrace. They could feel her trembling as she clutched them.

"I knew someone would come eventually but what took you so long?"

Mick kissed the top of her head. "We're sorry, baby. That storm came out of nowhere."

"You were in the boat with Jake, right?" Guil had by now joined them on the jetty. "Where is he?"

"There are two houses back there that got hit by mud. Dad, it was so scary. We were inside talking to a woman and her husband and we heard the sound of cracking trees. Luckily they knew what was happening and got us all outside. Lots of rocks came down too."

"But is everyone OK?"

"Yes. The young couple are desperate to get their baby somewhere warm for the night, so I've been running down every fifteen minutes or so to keep an eye out for any boats coming by. They have a car but don't want to risk driving out in case more mud comes down."

"Good thinking. Show us where they are."

Adele led the three men up a narrow road, away from the beach. The bush around them shook and dripped as they felt the ground under their feet incline.

Mick exhaled as they reached the top of the incline and came to a clearing where a rough, asphalt road terminated. "Oh my God, look at that."

Two houses faced each other across a divide of mud. One house seemed to have fared much better than the other; a thick stream of mud studded with rocks and small trees wrapped around from the back of the house and banked halfway up one exterior wall. From first sight it seemed all windows were still intact. The house opposite, however, was a huge, dripping mound. One side of the roof had collapsed, shards of corrugated iron protruding from the thick mud like lopsided candles on a melting birthday cake. A carport oozed mud that had pushed all of its contents (strangely enough, no car) out onto the street — recycling bins, a lawn mower, a fridge whose door had been severed and which hung at a weird angle off to one side.

"That's strange. Where have they gone?" murmured Adele. "They were standing right here."

Panicked voices came to them from somewhere above, obscured by dripping bush. The tarmacked road led away and sharply upwards under the escarpment. They started running, breathing deeply as the road inclined. Mick fell behind, feeling his pulse rocket.

Ethan, Guil and Adele bounded ahead and found Jake squatting in front of an upturned vehicle which had come to rest against a fallen tree trunk on the side of the road. Only the tyres were visible through a sticky coating of mud. Clicks of the disengaged engine could still be heard from underneath the slime. Jake was using a thick stump of a branch to help him scrape at the mud while a woman in a floral dressing gown stood and watched, rocking as the sound of a baby's whimpering came from beneath her robe.

Jake panted as they surrounded him. His eyes flashed relief at seeing them but his voice was tight and frantic. "He tried to drive away and more mud came down ... so fast ... we have to get him out ..."

Guil and Ethan looked around for something they could use to help while Adele put her arms around the rocking woman. Guil, having found nothing, simply squatted next to Jake and started pulling at the mud with both hands.

Mick limped over, taking in the scene. He rested with his hands on his knees as he looked from the car back to the escarpment shaking his head. "How could it *flip?*"

"Mate, can we please not analyse this now? Just *help!*"

Mick checked again nervously for any sign of more mud coming from above then squatted beside the passenger door on the opposite side from Jake.

The woman in the dressing gown whimpered. "We *told* him not to try to drive out. We knew the mud could come down! It's happened before. Always happens when it rains like this after a bad fire season."

"It's *never* rained like this," muttered Mick, scraping frantically at the door. "There's still a bit of mud coming down. If enough of it banks up against the car it might push it down the ravine. Can you feel how the car is sliding? We need to work fast."

The woman's voice rose in panic. "Why can't we hear anything from inside? Ben! *Ben*!" The newborn, who seemed to have drifted off to sleep, woke with its mother's cries and joined in with a shuddering wail.

"Please take them away," Jake whispered to Guil. "It's too much."

Guil wiped his hands off as best he could on his shorts and headed over to Adele and the sobbing woman. Adele had managed to coax the baby out of her arms. "Let's go and sit down," he said, pointing them in the direction of a flat boulder on the edge of the road around twenty metres back towards the house and away from the mudslide.

Adele cradled the small baby and offered it the back of her pinkie finger to suck. This bought them a few minutes of silence, interrupted only by the small, satisfied moans of the infant. Occasionally, realising it was being duped with a finger and frigid knuckle, the baby would pause and let out a high-pitched screech, only to search out Adele's wet pinkie again and latch on. The woman rocked and moaned. "He was just trying to get help. He wasn't running away ..."

Mick stopped his scraping and stood up, spreading his hands. "Shhh! Did you hear that?"

The scraping stopped and everyone held their breath.

"Did you hear it? He's alive!"

The woman started to weep with relief and Guil sprang up and ran over to the car, his fingers searching out the seam of the driver's door. Together, he and Jake managed to pull away enough mud to expose the door handle. Jake tugged and tugged but the weight of the mud oozing from the front of the car, which pointed up towards the escarpment, prevented him from being able to swing the door outwards. They tried to clear as much sludge as possible from the window but it remained streaked and opaque. They could not see inside and had no way of telling if any mud had seeped in.

"Guil, no! What are you doing?"

Guil had pulled himself up onto his feet and bent one leg behind him, the toe of his sneaker pointing at the window of the driver's door.

"Stop! His head might be just on the other side of the glass, don't kick it in!"

Guil kicked the window in a frenzy. It cracked but did not give. On the fourth or fifth kick, his foot slid along the mud-streaked glass, causing him to lose his balance and land on his hip on the road with a yelp. He had kicked with such force that the car pivoted on its roof and swung slowly in a clockwise direction towards Mick.

Jake stood over him. "What the fuck are you doing? You could have kicked his head in!" Ethan ran over to join Jake and they pulled Guil back and away from the car.

"Dad, break the window on your side!"

Mick was pushing with both hands against the car to stabilise its movement. "What good is that going to do? There is no way we'll be able to pull him across the car, especially if there's mud in there."

"You'll at least be able to reach in and make sure his head is out of the way while we break the window on this side. Find something to break it with. These windows are hard to smash in."

Mick stood and disappeared into the bush behind him, reemerging quickly with a large, flat stone grasped in his hands. He positioned himself awkwardly, like a child about to try ten-pin-bowling for the first time, swung the stone behind his hips, and then shoved it with as much force as he could through the window on the passenger side of the car. The glass shuddered before it broke into tiny crystals that scattered over his feet and the slippery ground. Mick then dropped to his knees, stuck his head through the cavity, and leaned into the car.

From inside they could hear Mick's muffled voice. "Go for it! His head is clear! And there's no mud in here, thank God!"

Jake ran around to Mick's side of the car and grabbed the stone, bringing it around to the driver's side of the car.

"Quick, quick!" Ethan was still restraining Guil. There had been no further sound from inside the car.

Jake swung the stone behind him and smashed through the glass. He and Ethan pulled the arms of their hoodies down to protect their fists and quickly cleared enough of the glass to make an opening. They each reached in and grabbed a shoulder, pulling on the limp body inside. The driver had not strapped himself in with the seatbelt and so had come to settle in a ball on the inverted roof of the car, his back to the window.

"Watch his neck if you can!" warned Adele from behind.

His body slid out relatively easily and they found a clear expanse of asphalt to stretch him out on. As Ethan pressed his fingers to the man's neck hoping to find a pulse, he felt hands pulling on his shirt.

"Let me take over," said Adele in a calm, steady voice. "I've practised this many times at Uni."

Ethan made room for Adele and stumbled towards the boulder, collapsing next to the woman who was taking the whole scene in with open-mouthed shock. Even the baby was silent as if sensing the importance of this moment. Ethan felt the adrenaline pulse through his body as he watched his sister bend over the man's face, her cheek turned towards his gaping mouth, hoping to feel breathe alight on her skin. After a few seconds she shook her head and announced; "We need to start CPR. Dad, you help me."

The small group listened to Adele's exaggerated exhalations and Mick's grunting as he pressed down through the heels of his hands onto the man's exposed thorax. At one point, the sickening sound of a rib cracking could be heard. Guil crawled away to retch under the cover of the surrounding bush.

. . . .

Mick steered the boat back into the bay, Ethan and Jake flanking him. Adele had the man they had resuscitated in the recovery position down in the cabin, his wife and baby anxiously perched next to him on the bench seats. Guil had pulled himself into a knot of limbs on the bench seat opposite, his face hidden.

The wind had died down so much the men on deck could speak without raising their voices. Some of the heavy cloud overhead had opened up, revealing bright patches of sky filled with the glowing stars of pre-dawn. Far in the distance, they could see the bright light of Mick's jetty beckoning them home.

Ethan rubbed his eyes, feeling exhausted now that the adrenaline had left his body. "That guy is so lucky he had a fairly new car. It was watertight. No mud got in at all."

"Yes and no. Those new cars have windows that are practically unbreakable. You saw how hard it was to get in to him. Imagine if you were alone and trying to get out!"

"What was that, a heart attack? He's a bit young for that, isn't he?"

Mick rubbed his eyes. "Adele told me sometimes a hard blow to the chest can cause that, even in a young person. He didn't have his belt on. Maybe he hit the steering wheel really hard when he flipped. Or maybe he was just terrified. I would have been."

Ethan leant towards his father. "By the way, what got into Guil? That was crazy, kicking at the window like that."

Mick shrugged. "I know. I was worried he would kick the car right off the edge of the road. The mud underneath and around the car was moving. That was a really hairy situation."

"It was like he was in a trance," agreed Jake.

From downstairs, Guil could hear the men talking softly. Although he couldn't make out the words clearly, he knew they were talking about him. His right leg and foot pulsed in pain. He had kicked at that window with wild panic as if it had been himself trapped inside, trying to get out. He had kicked with as much force as he wished he had used on that smoky day two years ago when he had watched his mother run into their home out west while black smoke billowed around their car. The irony was that *his* car door had not been locked on that day. All he would have needed to do was to reach out and open it and follow his mother inside to look for his father. How had he been able to access an extraordinary amount of energy just now to try to save a stranger, yet on the day that counted he had been frozen in place, unable to lift a finger? He was disgusted with himself, and ashamed at the blame he had been carrying for his mother. He vowed to tell her that as soon as he saw her.

He looked across at the faintly breathing man on the bench seat opposite, incredibly grateful he had not hurt him. The woman, still in her muddy, floral robe, looked with concern down at her husband as she cradled her baby in her arms.

You're lucky. He spoke the words inside his head. *Your family is still intact. Your baby will grow up with a father.*

When he started to sob, Adele leant over and put her arms around him, holding him as he shuddered with convulsions of tears. The dam was broken.

CHAPTER 18. ROOFTOP POOL

Sam wound her way barefoot through the sleeping bodies on her living room floor holding two mugs of coffee. Twelve air mattresses that had been hastily collected in the early hours of the morning were arranged in a star shape on the floor and piles of muddy clothes punctuated the space around them. Sam had tried to instil order when the boats had started coming back — and going again, and coming back — by ordering each muddy body to strip on the deck and leave their clothes in the laundry baskets she had provided. The sheer exhaustion of those returning to land had quickly overruled her pragmatism.

She handed one of the mugs to Mick, standing on the deck in the gentle glow of sunrise. His face reflected the weak light as he took in the muted lavender sky. Only the most feathery tendrils of thin cloud stretched over the bay now, high up and lightly moving away to the west and away from the beach, a delicate chiffon scarf being snatched away by an unseen hand. Down at the jetty, the five boats and Jet Ski were haphazardly tied onto the posts and to each other, clinking against each other like cubes of ice in a glass.

"Here, take this. This Moka pot really does make good coffee. Renata was right about that."

Mick wrapped his fingers around the mug with a sigh of gratitude. "Are they all asleep? How many did we end up with? I lost count."

"Around fifteen or sixteen. We have more upstairs. That's not counting the man Adele resuscitated. He and his family are still at the hospital."

"Hey, I was part of that resuscitation as well, you know."

"Yes. Adele told me you broke a rib."

"That happens sometimes. Better than dying, isn't it?" Mick sipped his coffee. "Everyone else OK?"

"Our crew are all fine. Thank God." Sam twisted around to take in the bodies on the mattresses behind her. Their soft snores wafted out to them. "Just a few deep cuts that needed to be looked at and one elderly lady who twisted her ankle running for the boat. The kids did so well. If they had not alerted the homes at the back to come forward and shelter there we might have been looking at a completely different situation. We bought them some time."

"We'll have to try to get back today and pick up more people. All the roads will be covered in mud by now. And some of the houses did go under from the storm surge at the waterfront. We need to check we really got to everyone. I hate to think of anyone stuck in their house waiting for help."

"You need to sleep first, Mick."

"No. I need to go and see Helen and check in with what happened to the apartment blocks. I'll bring over some more fuel for the boats. Guil said he had a stash in their garage. I hate to wake him but I need his help bringing it back over."

"And you'll want to check in on Renata."

Mick met Sam's eyes. He gently removed the empty coffee cup from her hand. "Get some rest. I'll bring back some food for everyone as well, if I can find anything open. I have no idea what we are going to find over there on the beach side this morning."

Mick circled the air mattresses until he found Guil. Only the most gentle tap on his shoulder was needed before he sprung up, disoriented. "Come on mate, let's go check on your mum."

Guil hastily pulled on his damp clothes, impregnated with the metallic stink of mud, and followed Mick out of the house. Mick threw some beach towels over the car seats and they cruised slowly through empty streets to the familiar crest at which the car veered to the right and the broad sweep of ocean was spread out before them. The two men took in the swollen volume of water and the sets of waves rolling in with mechanical regularity, no wind to distort and lash them into the frenzy of last night. Branches as thick as a child's arm had rained down over every surface. Garbage bins were upended and spilled their contents over the sodden lawns. Down in Bombora, some shopfronts had been hastily reinforced and concerned business owners were already out inspecting the damage, retrieving metal chairs and tables which had been scattered like dice throughout the mall.

"Let's park and walk along the Esplanade. I want to see which buildings, if any, got damaged. We can also drop in on Helen quickly before we go up to see your mum."

They parked in front of a cafe where a bewildered looking woman with fresh white sneakers and a Pomeranian on a leash peered through the closed glass doors. "Oooh, Mummy wanted a latte!" she whined to her dog, before looking sadly at Mick and Guil.

On their way down through the park, Mick nudged Guil onto the open stretch of grass which dipped down to the beach. "Let's avoid those pines lining the path. Any of the branches could be loose and about to fall." They came to the rock pool where only a few weeks ago Mick had hefted a baby shark over the wall and back into the ocean. They turned right, heading towards Vaga. As they passed the empty space they could see barricades still in place up ahead.

"There's no one here. Want to chance it? The surf is high but I think we can get around to your mum's place. I'm sure this is just a precaution."

"Let's do it."

They each skirted an end of the hastily installed barricade and started along the path. It was eerily quiet. Figures could be seen on a few balconies above them looking out to sea, clearly exhausted from a long night of staying hypervigilant as the storm raged. The path was wet and sediment had been dragged all the way to the grass under some of the low hanging balconies.

"It really came up," commented Mick. "I hope Helen is all right."

They rounded the point and took in the sight of the Palisade, glass doors glistening in the morning sun. They looked up at the top apartment and saw that the balcony door had been pulled wide open. She was awake. She was all right.

. . . .

Renata had not slept. Shortly after Mick and the boys had left, the rain seemed to drop in intensity so she took the opportunity to hurry over to Helen's home. She had helped Helen set a row of sandbags around the perimeter of the veranda and in front of the stairs leading up from the grass, both women struggling with the sodden bags. Renata had made Helen promise to call her if the water came up as high as the first step. "The first step, Helen! Not the second! Not the third!"

She had then returned home and made a nest of cushions for herself right on the floor in front of the balcony door and spent the night watching and listening to the waves. The meteorological drama shifted from the sky to the sea, the lightning a mere flutter in different corners of the sky and the thunder a low roll in the distance. The ocean, on the other hand, continued to thrash and whip in agitation.

She felt unusually calm in her apartment, listening to the boom of the waves far below, their spray occasionally carried high enough by the wind to smatter the glass in front of her face. She trusted the Palisade was set far enough back from the coast to be completely safe from the storm surge. Over at the Glades and Sunrise she could see the blinking lights of the Emergency Services in the car parks at the back of the two buildings. She assumed they were on standby in case an evacuation was needed. Mick had been right — they were focusing all their attention on the eastern side of the peninsula and probably would not have had any leftover capacity to send back into the national park and the small communities of the inlets.

Despite feeling apprehensive that Guil was still out in the storm, even though it had eased off quite a bit in the early hours of the morning, she had allowed herself to feel stirrings of pride at all they had been able to set in motion in the last couple of days. All of it had started with her son and his fledgling efforts to gather a loose group of volunteers to be at the ready in case of an extreme weather event, which Mick had picked up on and amplified.

Mick. He had been a complete revelation. When she had first met him again after returning to Bombora, she had assumed he was full of talk and empty assurances after she had voiced her concerns about squatters and the safety of the Palisade. She had never really lost her scepticism that somehow all of his actions were solely aimed at winning her over, a way for him to flaunt his resources and local clout as a part of an elaborate mating game. After their unexpected tryst on the rooftop, she had wondered if he might walk back his offers of help; instead, he had doubled down. To see the way he had sprung into action at the storm's violent landfall had taken away any doubt she had.

However, it was his gentle treatment of Sam when she had reappeared suddenly the day before the storm that had deeply moved her. Despite the intense awkwardness of the situation — of which Sam did not know the details, but which Renata knew she could definitely sense — Mick was fair and kind, even inviting Sam into the heart of their mission. The three of them had moved cautiously around one another, but Mick had taken every opportunity to meet Renata's gaze or brush against her hand and to silently let her know that it was she he would come looking for after the storm.

Just before sunrise, her phone had pinged and she read Mick's message that the last of the boats had returned and they were all going to try to grab some sleep. All the residual tension left her body and she relaxed into her cushions, yet still she could not drift off into sleep. She would wait for Guil to come home. The rising sun warmed her cheek, slowly moved over her face and up to her hairline. Soon she was lying in a bright puddle of sunlight, enjoying the deep quiet of her apartment and the softening of her muscles in the intensified warmth radiating through glass. When her hips finally protested against lying on the hard floor with only thin cushions beneath her, she stretched, pulled open the sliding door for some fresh air, and headed towards her bedroom for a change of clothes.

Just as she passed the kitchen island, she was surprised to step directly into a puddle of water. Her first thought was that Guil had crept in without her having heard him and had trailed water with him through the apartment. *How strange. Surely I would have heard him.*

A drop of water landed squarely in the centre of the puddle. Renata lifted her face to the ceiling. Two more drops spattered down onto her cheek in quick succession causing her to blink rapidly in confusion. Simultaneously, she heard voices rising in alarm in the apartment next door and the sound of water smacking onto the tiled floor of her bathroom. She poked her head around the bathroom door and was horrified to see the plaster roof above her toilet swollen and emitting a single and constant rivet of water.

Her thoughts flew back to the night on the rooftop with Mick. As they had headed back towards the stairwell holding hands, they had giggled as they dodged broad puddles of water, Mick helping Renata to spring over them with his good hand. It only occurred to her now to wonder why there was so much water up there when it hadn't rained for at least several days. With a sickening dread in her stomach, she recalled the papers she had been sorting in Mick's living room. She struggled to recall; something about the roof here at the Palisade? And she had told Mick not to prioritise it, to concentrate on the buildings closer to the coast?

Realising she was wearing nothing more than a t-shirt and a pair of underpants, she rushed into her bedroom and grabbed a pair of jeans. Without stopping to pull them on, she ran for her front door, snatching up her wallet and phone from the kitchen bench out of instinct. She made it into the hall and started running barefoot towards the elevator, then stopped and pivoted. Elevator or stairwell? She ran towards the same grey door that she had taken Mick through just two nights before.

She had made it down one flight of stairs before a wall of water gushed down behind her, sweeping her off her bare feet. Her body slipped under the bottom rung of the railing into the long, concrete shaft of the stairwell, and was carried by a thick cascade of water to the very bottom.

. . . .

Mick and Guil homed in towards the beacon of Renata's apartment, falling into companionable silence, a sense of the worst being over and disaster averted. Guil knew he was too tired to put into words the apology he felt he owed his mother but looked forward to hugging her; Mick simply looked forward to delivering Renata's most precious person back to her intact, as promised, and seeing one of the rare but beautiful smiles break out over her face.

A horrendous crack sounded out in the still morning, intruding on their solitary thoughts. The men lifted their eyes from the path they were ambling along to the general direction of the Palisade, from where the sound of splintering and tearing was coming. By the time their eyes found the precise epicentre of the dreadful sound, water erupted suddenly from every window on the Palisade's top floor, punching out the glass panes and ejecting thick torrents of water in all directions. Glass wheeled through the air like terrible frisbees and shattered on the ground below. It only took a few seconds for the full load of water, which had collected all night on the flat roof of the building, to flush through the top floor apartments, a shocking and forceful enema. Just as suddenly as it had started, it reduced quickly to a dribble running down the sides of the building, bringing household items and debris down with it.

The men stood rooted to the spot for several seconds, unable to comprehend what they had just witnessed. Mick's hand instinctively reached to block Guil's body, the same way a parent stretches out an arm over a child when having to brake suddenly while driving.

Silence gave way to screaming coming from all directions.

Faces pressed against the glass doors below Renata's apartment before quickly disappearing. Bodies appeared on the balconies of the surrounding apartment blocks, hands clutching shocked faces. The double glass doors at the base of the Palisade were thrown open and the residents started to spew out onto the grass, running away from the building and taking up positions not far from Guil and Mick on the Esplanade, staring in disbelief at the water still dribbling down the walls. House plants plopped with wet thuds onto the grass.

A dining chair had come to rest upside down in the broad fan of a palm tree. A living room rug was now draped over a balcony on the second floor. Other items of furniture studded the perimeter of the building. A television screen had exploded with a bang on the pavement in front of Helen's house, causing her to rush out in a dressing gown, clutching her cup of tea. She saw Guil and rushed over, grabbing his hand and staring with him in the direction of his apartment. There was a gaping hole where the sliding balcony glass doors had been. Guil shook his head and started to crumple towards the pavement.

"No, no, no ... "

"Stay with him," Mick whispered to Helen. "Don't let him come closer."

Feeling nauseous, Mick started to pick his way around the building, deliberately choosing to go anti-clockwise and thereby putting off walking directly under Renata's apartment right away. He kept his eyes to the ground, sodden and squelching with every one of his footfalls. Mechanically, he stepped carefully over books, smashed photo frames, vases, plates, cutlery, shoes. He thought he might collapse when passing a shattered crib. Empty, thank God.

His heart raced as he rounded one, and then a second corner, forcing his shaking legs to keep going. He needed to do this for Guil.

He stopped suddenly at the sight of a shattered terracotta pot with a rosemary bush spilling from between its broken shards. He started to cry then, remembering that when Renata had bent to kiss him, she had tasted both of Madeira wine and rosemary. An image of her thoughtfully stroking her upper lip with her sprig of rosemary as they stood together on the rooftop two nights before, an electrical storm far out at sea charging the air between them, swam before his eyes. He had to force himself to keep moving when all he wanted to do was lie in the wet grass and scream.

He completed his reconnaissance mission around the building. There were no bodies. The area under Renata's apartment was scattered only with the same household debris he had found on the other sides of the building.

A man yelled from a balcony above. "We can't use the stairwell to get down, it's filled with water up to the first floor!"

Mick called up in a trembling voice. "We'll get someone up to you soon, mate." He made his way back to Guil and Helen on shaking legs.

"We need to go sit down," whispered Mick to Helen.

Guil's shock made him compliant and malleable as they each gently pressed on a shoulder and guided him towards Helen's home, the perimeter still studded with the sandbags Renata had helped position mere hours before. Guil collapsed onto the steps. Helen made tea which no one drank, and they listened to the sirens coming closer and closer from the veranda of Renata's favourite house on the Esplanade.

CHAPTER 19. AFTERMATH

The house was finally still. Mick found Sam in the kitchen, idly stirring a tea.

"All asleep?" she asked.

"Your mum's light is out."

Barb had not yet gone back to the nursing home, although a week after the storm they had opened their doors again. They had experienced light flooding around the entrance from a burst pipe but there had been no serious damage. Sam was finding it so comforting to have her mother with her all day that she ended up leaving the Airbnb and coming back to the house, preferring to sleep in Adele's bedroom while her mother stayed in the guest bedroom next door. Her mother had camped out on the couch while she watched Sam battle with a steam cleaner for days trying to get mud stains out of her springy beige carpets. "You know what Mum, I would be happy to just rip all this damn carpet up and have floorboards," she had muttered in exasperation. "I might finally have my way with this house yet!"

Sam pushed her teacup away and met Mick's eyes. "Hear anything from upstairs?" She meant Ethan's old room, where Guil had reluctantly taken up residence. Immediately after the storm and the collapsed roof of the Palisade, he had gone to stay with Jake, terrifying both his friend and his parents with his moroseness. His grief was a dark cloud that hung around him and made him sleep around the clock. Mick had popped over to visit him a couple of times and been sent away, not before Jake had told him that he had barely eaten and had stopped going to school.

"It's not working out, Mick. We don't have a spare room so he's been on the couch, but he sleeps all day. My mum is losing it."

Mick had spoken to Sam and they had both agreed to offer him Ethan's room, which had its own separate entrance. "You can be as independent as you like. We can bring food up to you or you are welcome to come down to eat with us. Whatever you want, Guil."

Guil could barely look Mick in the eye but desperately wanted his own space where he would not be disturbed or made to feel bad about not wanting to shower, dress, or socialise. Since he had moved in they had not seen him, but they heard footfalls and the sliding open and close of windows in their frames. Sam dropped bags of groceries in front of the door with a notepad where he could write down anything he needed.

"Do we need to tell the authorities that he is with us? I mean technically he is a minor, right? He has to either be with family or go into some sort of care?"

"I'm not sure what happens to a teenager as old as he is. It would be good to be able to sit down and talk to him about what he wants, but understandably he doesn't want to speak to me right now. He has no more direct family in Bombora. I think Renata had mentioned paternal grandparents out west."

Speaking Renata's name out loud caused them to both stare hard at the marble kitchen island, both lost in their own thoughts. Sam took a deep breath. "Why do you feel so connected to him,

Mick? You only knew him and his mother for such a short time. What was the exact nature of your relationship with her?"

"Come on, we both knew Renata as kids. You know I've always been someone to help any local out whenever I could. And he's just a kid, an orphan now. How could anyone turn their back on him?" He paused and took a shaky breath. "Let's not even mention the fact that if it wasn't for me ... well, I feel responsible for what happened at the Palisade."

"The investigation will clear that up, Mick. The real estate agent hadn't reported the roof leaks to you, and when you found out it was too late. No one will be able to prove negligence. I am sure of it."

"Well whether they prove it or not, in Guil's mind I am well and truly responsible. And it's not just the roof they are investigating. It's also how she managed to fit under the rail at all ..." At this point Mick's voice wavered and he quickly turned his back, swinging open the fridge door and pretending to search its contents. Sam waited until he pivoted back towards her, empty-handed.

"He's just angry at the whole world right now. He's angry at everyone who has a mother or a father, or a sister or brother for that matter. It will take a while before he is ready to start processing all of this."

Mick had barely set eyes on him since the roof collapse. A friend of his at the morgue had called him to tell him that despite having called the next of kin repeatedly, no one had been up to identify Renata's body. Mick had driven over to Jake's and spoken to Guil through the screen door.

"I can drive you up, Guil. I can wait for you outside and bring you straight back."

In the end, Guil had been unable to leave the house and Mick had been the one to identify Renata. He had shaken so much on being escorted through the frigid corridors of the morgue that his friend had needed to physically support him.

"Let's do this as quickly as possible, mate."

His friend had peeled the black cover down to Renata's bare shoulders. Mick had not needed long. The arched eyebrows, the high cheekbones. Only one ugly bruise near her temple marred her skin, no longer olive but a cool porcelain. Her thick hair had been scraped back and secured behind her head. He realised he had never seen her with her hair back like that. She had always preferred to wear it loose around her face and spilling over her shoulders, twisting it around one finger when she was thoughtful, exactly as she had done during exams at school while Mick watched her surreptitiously from the back row of the classroom.

He had forced himself to ask his friend how many other bodies had been brought in from the Palisade.

"Four."

He had been unable to speak to Sam about how sick he had felt visiting the morgue. He had also had to drive back to Guil and let him know that the only choice they had was to cremate Renata, unless he wanted to bury her outside of Bombora. His most horrible premonition had come true; the cemetery had flooded so badly during the storm that it would have been impossible to lay Renata to rest there. The whole area had been closed off and the water that refused to drain away was being tested every day for contamination. On top of everything, Guil had to imagine the effect that the flooding was having on the resting place of his maternal grandparents.

No investigation could mete out a punishment to Mick that was worse than having to speak those words through the screen door to an unresponsive Guil.

Sam saw how tortured Mick was. She stopped pressing him about his relationship to Renata, and busied herself in the house that was now suddenly full of people. Since the storm, Adele and Ethan popped over more frequently. She suspected that Ethan was keen to keep an eye on Guil and make sure he knew that he was a temporary guest in his old bedroom, and Adele was keen to keep an eye on Sam and make sure she wasn't sedating herself every evening with wine.

She needn't have worried. Sam was busier than ever, catering to a steady flow of people coming to the house. As news of the tinnie army spread through Bombora, more and more of their neighbours came by with ideas for future volunteer efforts, starting with the massive cleanup that needed to take place throughout the peninsula. Every part of it had been damaged in some way. To Sam's surprise, she emerged as a natural leader in Mick's absence, coordinating volunteers and spearheading new initiatives. She relished the new feeling of being of service to her community. Even Barb commented with a sly grin behind the rim of her teacup, "Now that Mick's out of action, look at you go!"

It was true that Mick was mentally exhausted and completely distracted by the investigation into the roof collapse. To her surprise, he often sought her out in the kitchen for advice and reassurance. She had never seen him so humble and vulnerable, yet she was confident he would get through the investigation and then ultimately get over the worst of his grief. She knew it would not be long before he was back hatching plans to protect Bombora and locking horns with Rodney at the local council.

She was sure of this because now he had one overriding reason to do so; Renata had loved Bombora as much as they both did. For that very reason alone, it was worth protecting.

Every night she went to bed in Adele's bed sensing her husband, her mother, and now Guil partitioned off in their own bedrooms throughout the house, each person alone with their own thoughts and struggles and facing the demons of the night. She had to deal with the initial excruciating sting of feeling like she had won some kind of race with an unfair advantage. She had to admit her life was complex and this constellation that had bloomed around her surprised her as much as anyone, but she no longer cared what anyone thought. She didn't care how it looked that she had taken in the son of a woman who everyone whispered had been with Mick. Her relationship with him was her business and she owed it to no one to make it conventional.

Whenever Sam's motivation wavered, she would creep into her old bedroom and look at the lacquered box of aspirin. *That's not me anymore.* She would not drink away her boredom, nor would she run to the next retreat in search of answers. Regardless of what happened with Mick, she had found a purpose. More correctly, she had stopped running and it had finally found her.

. . . .

Guil curled up into a ball in Ethan's large box spring bed. He had never lain in a bed quite so soft and pliable yet it did nothing to help him sleep. He lay awake most of the night staring at Ethan's desk opposite the bed, illuminated from the light of the ensuite bathroom which he never turned off. There was a huge pin wall full of clippings of modern architecture behind a collection of several 3D models. Sprawling houses with intricate decks and garden terraces. Bungalows. No high-rise apartment blocks with flat roofs.

He went over and over the words he had planned to say to his mother. That he too had been in an emergency and acted in a way he could not comprehend. That he could understand now that she had had a singular focus on the afternoon of the fire, to protect her son, and that her tunnel vision meant that she could not read all the signals around her, just like the man in the car had blocked out the obvious warning signs in an attempt to access help and driven out on to a road already slick with mud. Guil would never be able to make amends for the last time they had spoken of the fire. It had been clear, although unspoken, that he blamed her for the death of his father. She had died thinking that.

He knew he could not hide out in this room forever. As much as he tried to despise Mick, he couldn't. He had seen his mother bloom in the weeks before she died, and he knew Mick was the reason for that. He did not want to go out west to his father's parents where the scene of the fire was just a short walk away. Renata had hated it out west and he would have felt like a traitor going back out there. The best thing he could do, he decided, was finish school. His friends from school were contacting him daily and asking when he would be coming back. Renata was very much her parents' child and shared the immigrant's love of hard work and enterprise; she would have been devastated to see him drop out now, so close to his final exams. It was the only way he could think of to honour her memory.

In two months he would turn eighteen, and his high school graduation was three months after that. By then, he hoped to have formed a plan for what came next.

EPILOGUE. GUIL

A year has passed since the storm. Guil stands with his feet in the ocean, the water lapping gently and quietly between and around his toes, barely making a noise as it rustles over and through a thin layer of broken shells.

He cannot not know that five and a half thousand kilometres south of where he stands, an ice mass the size of five Switzerlands and two kilometres deep is being hollowed out from beneath by abnormally warm waters, becoming as porous as honeycomb. Soundless, irreversible, and invisible. Even if he were to stand right on top of it, not one of his five senses would detect this decay, the precarious thinness beneath the deceptive bulk. Soon, it will collapse with a roar, spilling ice cubes into the ocean which will be pushed around faster and faster by the swirling eddies and currents, hastening their demise. He doesn't know any of this, nor what a dramatic and permanent effect this will have on the water level off the Australian coast and elsewhere, but he feels something is terribly amiss. He stares at the tiny bubbles skitting gently over his toenails and knows not to be lulled into a sense of false security.

He thinks about the role the ocean has played in his family's life.

His great grandfather, evacuated from Gibraltar to Madeira during the Second World War to be out of the Germans' path, would have thought of the ocean primarily as a liquid highway, a means of getting as quickly as possible from point A to point B and from danger to safety. This highway had served him dutifully again when he brought his new bride from Madeira to mainland Portugal, both of them peeling oranges on the deck of the polished wooden carrack, knowing that when they started to see clouds of glossy gulls wheeling in the air above them they were close to their new home.

For his maternal grandparents, the oceans were impossibly large splotches of cobalt blue on a double-paged map spread on their laps while they took in the distance between Lisbon and Sydney. His grandmother had cried as his grandfather traced the route with his finger, patting her knee and promising to work hard to give her life of comfort and leisure.

"I need to see the ocean every day," she had sobbed. "Don't make me live in the middle of that huge country." The sheer difference in size between Portugal — a thin sliver of land clinging to Spain — and Australia, audaciously claiming the bottom right-hand corner of the entire map and illustrated in the garish colours of a fresh sunburn, terrified her. The ocean would be her touchstone, the one thing that would be similar between her life in Lisbon and the life awaiting her so far away. She would cling like a barnacle to the coast down there in the corner (she tapped her finger over the New South Wales coast line), the same way Portugal clung to the European continent.

His father. Guil's earliest memories were of being held safely in his muscular arms as his father either strode into the ocean or out of it again, shining with the briny water. He can still feel the secure grip of his father's arms and his vigorous heartbeat pulsing steadily in his strong, bare chest. Nothing felt better than being enclosed in that warm nest from which he would extend a chubby leg to feel the mysterious, cold water with a toe. His father would gently lower him into the salty water, keeping one huge hand spread under his tiny shoulder blades and supporting him to float, using his other hand to scoop water gently over his belly. When he was older, the water play became rougher; his father would dunk, throw and catapult him through and over the ocean with Renata watching intently from a picnic rug on the sand. His father taught him to use the force of the ocean to do extraordinary, athletic things. Body surfing, then real surfing. He also taught Guil about its dangers; how to spot a rip tide, and why you should never surf for at least three days after a long period of rain. *"You'll get sicker than a dog if you do that. All the nasty bacteria and poo gets swept into the ocean."*

He learned from his father the restorative powers of the salt and waves. From a very young age, Guil could see that his father moved inexplicably through many moods in one day, but he observed that he always returned from a swim or a surf feeling calmer and more settled. In fact, Renata would send him out to the beach when things were tense or his father was starting to pace like a caged tiger in their small flat. Up until the day of the cliff incident his father was in the ocean practically every day, even if it was a quick five-minute dip before or after work. It was not unusual to see him at the breakfast table with wet hair stinking of salt and brine, summer or winter. That is, until the day the ocean showed a side to him he had never seen — sucking, spitting, spewing, screaming — as he hung suspended in a harness next to the wreckage of a human being that his own shaking, gloved hands had packed together. He never recovered from the betrayal of the ocean as it grabbed organs and soft tissue from the rocks and swept them out of his reach, hungry and indifferent to human suffering and to the mission he had been sent to complete. After that day, his father turned his back on the ocean, heartbroken but resolute, like when a lifelong friend surprises you with such toxic vitriol that you have no choice but to distance yourself. Even when they come back promising to be better, kinder — you have seen what you have seen. Ignore it at your own peril. Raise the drawbridge. Create a safe distance.

And now his mother. How she had suffered when his father insisted they put so many kilometres between themselves and the coast. In his need to create safe distance from the fickle waters, his father had condemned Renata to the static and shrivelling heart of New South Wales, a place on the map that his grandmother had despaired over and was as equally feared by Renata in a form of intergenerational symbiosis. Renata needed the rhythms of the ocean to feel safe and connected to her parents and beyond that, to their history — love matches and the proud pursuit of better opportunities, the chance to work hard and provide a good life, all facilitated and made possible by a generous, magnanimous ocean. Even when the storm hit, Renata was incapable of thinking the ocean would turn on her. She had felt safe in her apartment, even slightly thrilled by the sudden swelling and operatic howling of the water as it slammed into the rock platforms of Bombora, a watery magnet holding her in place. To be precise, it was not the ocean that had killed her — she had not been betrayed by her great love — not directly, anyway. The volume of water that pooled on the Palisade's roof — over eighty centimetres in two hours — obviously originated from the ocean, having been sucked up by unusually warm and humid weather in the days before the storm. *Let's not nitpick,* thought Guil.

So now Guil has to decide what the ocean is to him. Friend, foe, joy, terror, home? Playground or insatiable burial ground? A vicious protagonist of the ages, or an innocent victim, itself suffering under the planet's unstoppable warming? Something to run away from, like that toxic friend that turns? Or his family touchstone, never to be left again?

The soft, prickling water danced over his toes in complete indifference to his musings. In the time that it has taken to think these thoughts, the five-Switzerland-sized ice cube has been further hollowed out, the porous honeycomb growing a few more tiny chambers.

The ocean will swell and consume land, not because she has a will or a desire to do so. Guil stands alone, first fatherless and now motherless, but he cannot vilify the ocean for that.

He turns and sees the outline of Mick up on the Esplanade outside Vaga, true to its name, completely vacant except for the glistening, curved bar that was made with hardworking, proud Portuguese hands.

Mick lifts a hand which is holding his thongs and swings them in the air, calling to Guil.

"Come on, mate!"

There is so much work to do.

ACKNOWLEDGEMENTS

Like many, the effects of climate change are far from abstract to me. I see their ever-increasing impact in the world around me but most strikingly, I see how it is starting to insidiously affect the place I was born on the east coast of Australia. I started writing this book in April 2022 after an Australian summer marked by perpetual heavy rain and then huge flooding events near and around Lismore and Byron Bay, when a great many lives were saved by untrained citizens using the equipment they had to hand — Jet Skis, paddle boards, and small aluminium boats with outboard motors called "tinnies". The phrase "tinnie army" was born to describe the bravery of these first responders and, to me, symbolises the grit, determination and compassion of the Australian character that I am so proud of. This book is dedicated to those Australians who stepped up to supplement the official emergency services to save so many lives. I fear that these natural events will only accelerate over time and we as a community need to be ready to stand together and look out for each other's safety.

Of course, I would be remiss not to personally thank my family who enthusiastically encouraged me, brainstormed with me, read early pages, and constantly asked me if I was finished yet. There have also been several very dear friends throughout my life, who, every time I met them, would ask me: "And are you writing yet?" Thank you for never letting me forget the storyteller residing inside me and for giving me the courage to unleash her.

ABOUT THE AUTHOR

Vanessa Lee is an author and poet whose heart and imagination straddle two continents. Raised in a beachside community on Australia's East Coast, today she lives in Europe where she is at her happiest when hiking the solitary Alpine peaks of Italy, Switzerland and Austria with her family — this is also the environment where she feels most creative. Her stories and poems weave her own memories and love for her country of birth together with the sense of expansion and adventure she has found in the diversity of Europe.

.

Printed in Great Britain
by Amazon

33378773R00133